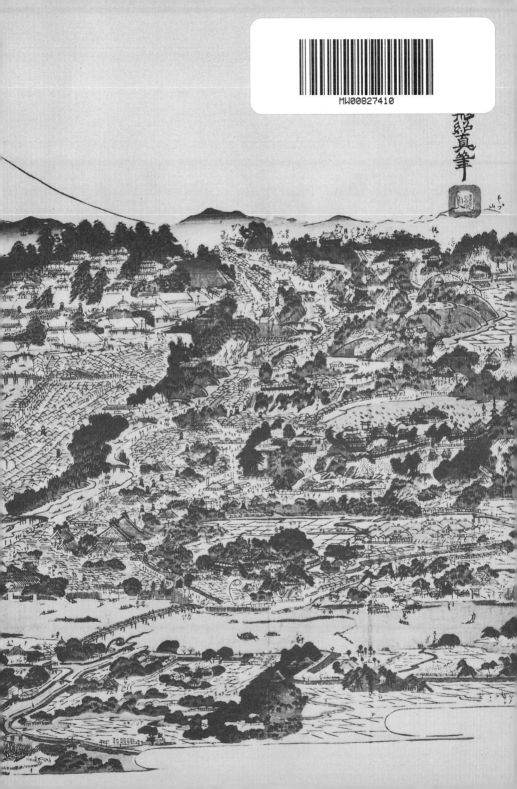

MASTER ASSASSIN

MASTER ASSASSIN

Tales of Murder from the Shogun's City

Shotaro Ikenami

Translated by Gavin Frew

KODANSHA INTERNATIONAL
New York • Tokyo • London

Originally published by Kodansha, Ltd. under the
title *Koroshi no Yonin*.

Distributed in the United States by
Kodansha America, Inc.,
114 Fifth Avenue, New York, N.Y. 10011, and in the
United Kingdom and continental Europe by
Kodansha Europe, Ltd., Gillingham House,
38–44 Gillingham Street, London SW1V 1HU.

Published by Kodansha International Ltd.,
17–14 Otowa 1-chome, Bunkyo-ku, Tokyo 112, and
Kodansha America, Inc.

91 92 93 94 10 9 8 7 6 5 4 3 2 1
ISBN 4–7700–1534–8

Library of Congress Cataloging-in-Publication Data
Ikenami, Shotaro, 1923-1990
   [*Koroshi no yonin*. English]
   Master Assassin: Tales of Murder from the Shogun's City
Shotaro Ikenami : translated by Gavin Frew
   p.   cm.
   Translation of : *Koroshi no yonin*
   I. Title.
PL853. K4K8413 1991
895.6'35—dc 20

                                 91-14799
                                 CIP

CONTENTS

TWO WIVES

Despite his wife's warnings, Kinzo the clogmaker got out of bed to have a smoke. He had managed to do without his pipe during his illness, but now that he was feeling a little better, the urge was too powerful to resist. Waiting until his wife, Odai, had gone out on an errand, he walked unsteadily down the street to buy some tobacco, then ransacked the house looking for the pipe she had hidden.

When Odai got back home, their five-year-old daughter strapped to her back, she could hardly believe her eyes.

"What are you doing?" she said, trying to grab the pipe from his hand. "You mustn't let Dr. Baian catch you smoking."

"Leave me alone. A few puffs on a pipe never hurt anyone."

He pushed her away and continued to smoke. He was

9

still very pale, his eyes puffy from the illness.

At that moment Baian came through the back door. He silently walked up behind Kinzo and struck him on the back of the head. As Kinzo doubled over, clutching his head, Baian snatched the pipe from his hand, snapped it in two, and put the pieces into his kimono together with the remaining tobacco.

Baian was a huge man, over six feet tall, but he moved with an easy grace that denied his bulk. His eyes were small slits hidden beneath jutting brows, and sometimes it was difficult to tell whether they were open or closed. His head was shaven in the manner of most doctors in those days.

Nobody knew much about his private life, but there was no shortage of rumors about him.

"They say that he trained in Kyoto."

"You'd never think that a man of his size with such thick fingers could work so delicately."

"He moves so slowly that sometimes it scares me to watch him work."

"Yes, but he certainly knows what he's doing."

"You can say that again. I had this trouble with my back for three months, but he cured me in five days."

"As quickly as that?"

"Yes, but he has to be in the right mood to see you—if he doesn't feel like working, nothing will change his mind. He's a strange one, that Baian. Did you know that while he's treating his patients he never says a word?"

On this occasion, however, the usually taciturn Baian was quick to speak.

"Have you forgotten you almost died the other day? Your wife didn't sit by you day and night just to watch you kill yourself as soon as you begin to feel a bit better. If you start smoking again, you won't last another three days."

Baian spoke quietly, but as he listened, Kinzo began to tremble.

After Baian had gone, Kinzo turned to Odai and said, "Did you hear his voice? It put the fear of God in me."

"What do you mean? He just mumbled under his breath as he usually does."

"No, he was terrifying. I thought he was going to kill me."

"Don't be stupid. But he made sense, you know. No more tobacco for you."

"All right, have it your way."

From that moment on, Kinzo lay quietly in bed and did exactly as his wife told him. Odai did not think there was anything frightening about the way Baian had spoken to her husband, but she was grateful for the effect he had had on him. All she wanted was for him to get well as soon as possible, so he could get back into his shop and work again.

Kinzo's house stood halfway up the hill leading to Shinagawadai. In those days the area was still a suburb of Edo, commanding good views to the south and west over fields and woodland. Temples, farmhouses, and the mansions of lords and samurai dotted the wooded hillsides.

A little further to the south was a shrine called Kijinomiya. Tradition held that, at the beginning of the century, the shogun had been hunting in the area when a pheasant flew into the shrine in order to escape. The shogun asked some locals what the shrine was called. When told that it did not have a name, he declared that from that day forth it would be known as Kijinomiya—the Shrine of the Pheasant.

Nestling in the woods on the other side of the stream that flowed past the shrine's gateway was the small thatched house where Baian lived.

11

Although Baian looked over forty, he was in fact only thirty-five. He lived alone without assistants. His only help was Oseki, the wife of a local farmer, who came in to do his cleaning and laundry.

Baian returned from his house calls that day to find a basket of fish by the front door. Although basically an easygoing man not very interested in money or material possessions, he was a highly skilled doctor who often received simple gifts from his patients, which would seem to indicate that, despite his brusque manner, he was well-liked. He never took on cases he knew to be beyond his skills, and though it broke his heart to turn his back on people in pain, he would simply recommend that they see a better doctor.

He carried the fish to the kitchen, smacking his lips in anticipation. It was just after the New Year, and winter was the best time of the year for fish.

He poured some soy sauce and *sake* into a pan, then added the fish to stew. When they were ready he carried them to the table and poured himself a generous helping of cold *sake* before settling down to eat.

The heavy clouds that had covered the sky since morning produced an occasional flurry of snow, and though it was only four in the afternoon he was forced to light a lamp before eating his meal.

"Excuse me," a gruff voice called from the front door. "Is Dr. Baian at home?"

Baian gulped down the remainder of the *sake* before answering.

"Is that you, Ichibei? Come in," he called out without getting up from the table.

Like Baian, Ichibei was a large man. His manner was extremely polite, and in his expensive clothes he looked like a wealthy storekeeper or merchant.

He walked into the room and sat down at the table opposite Baian. "It's started to snow again," he said.

"You shouldn't have come out in weather like this."

"That's all right, I've got a palanquin waiting for me at a teahouse down the road."

"What can I do for you?"

"Need you ask? I come to see you only for one reason. There's someone I'd like you to take care of for me."

Despite his respectable appearance, Ichibei was a powerful underworld boss who controlled the brothels in the city-center district of Akasaka. He was over sixty, but the hand that placed thirty-five gold pieces on the table in front of Baian seemed that of a much younger man. He peered into Baian's face, trying to gauge his reaction.

Baian reached out lazily, counted the coins, and then nodded.

"You'll do it then?"

"You'd better tell me a bit more about the job first."

"It's a woman."

"A woman?"

"There is a large restaurant in Yagenbori called the Manshichi. I want you to kill the owner's wife."

Baian said nothing and his face remained expressionless, but he was startled. Three years earlier he had been paid fifty gold pieces to kill the owner's previous wife. Of course, Ichibei would not know anything about that. On that occasion, it had been Kahei, boss of the Honjo area, who had retained his services.

Baian did not mention any of this to Ichibei; it had no bearing on the present job, and in his trade, the only things that determined whether or not he accepted a job were the amount he was to be paid and who the go-between was. The identity of the victim was quite irrelevant. Both Ichibei and Kahei were clients in whom Baian felt he could have complete trust.

Baian thought for a short while, then he reached out to pick up the money, which represented half his fee, and slipped it inside his kimono.

Ichibei smiled happily. "There's no hurry on this one. I know I can trust you to do a neat job," he said, getting up from the table.

The Rules of the Game

When a professional killer like Baian was hired to murder someone, two other people were always involved. First was the person who had made the original request and paid the money. Second was the go-between—an underworld boss like Ichibei, who kept several hired killers on call and arranged for the job to be done. The hired killer never met the person who paid for the murder, and he left it to the go-between to look into the job and make the final decision as to whether the victim deserved to die.

The go-between was never actually involved in the execution of the murder, he simply handed it over to a suitable professional. But he had to be very careful about which jobs he accepted, because he often posed a respectable member of society and could not afford to be implicated in a murder.

Hired killers were in the job only for the money, and so they did not bother themselves with the details; in fact they were not allowed to know anything apart from their victim's identity. They had to have perfect trust in the go-between. For his services, the go-between took half the fee and passed the remainder on to the hired killer.

A large number of murders were committed in Edo, and it would be no exaggeration to say that most of them were committed by hired killers like Baian. Two hundred years ago forensic science was undreamed of, and because a professional left no clues behind to point to murder, there was little the authorities could do.

That night Baian lay in bed, wondering who had paid for the murder of the owner's first wife, and who could want to see his second wife dead. It was extremely rare for something like this to happen: a contract taken out on the two wives of the same man, and the same assassin employed to do both jobs. Baian felt there was more to this job than met the eye. As a rule, a hired killer did not bother himself with something as trivial as motive, but in this case Baian could not help becoming interested.

Most hired killers shrank from murdering women, but as long as the money was good enough, Baian did not have such scruples.

There was only one person Baian trusted sufficiently to discuss his work with: his friend and fellow assassin, Hikojiro. But Hikojiro would never take on a job like this.

"I don't know how you can do it, Baian," Hikojiro said. "I could never kill a woman."

"Nonsense. A woman is much easier to kill than a man. Men usually have some saving graces, but women—women are all evil at heart."

❖ ❖ ❖

Two days after Ichibei's visit, Baian left the house early in the morning.

"I might be gone for two or three days," he told Oseki as he left.

Baian arrived in Yagenbori a little after noon and went to the Manshichi for lunch. He was wearing an expensive silk kimono under a black jacket and a pale greenish-yellow cloth hat. He looked impressive, and anyone who saw him would immediately assume that he was a famous doctor.

Yagenbori took its name from a canal built to ferry rice to the government storehouses. The canal had been filled in fifty years before, and the area was now famous for its restaurants and pleasure houses. The present owner of the Manshichi was a man in his fifties called Zenshiro; the restaurant had been in his family for four generations.

When Baian had last visited the restaurant three years earlier, it had been packed with customers. Admittedly that had been in the evening, but all the same he was amazed to see how much it had changed. Yagenbori was even more popular nowadays, but for some reason the boom seemed to have passed by the Manshichi. Although it was lunchtime, there were few other customers, and even the private room in which Baian sat seemed gloomy.

It's a strange thing about the restaurant business, Baian mused, but when the owner is fully in charge and the staff is working happily, there is a feeling of prosperity about the place. On the other hand, once business starts to fall off, even the walls and fittings seem to lose their sheen, and the atmosphere becomes oppressive.

A waitress came into the room with a flask of *sake*.

"You don't seem to be very busy today," Baian commented.

"No, sir," she answered a little embarrassed.

She had a good figure and seemed pleasant enough, with large dark eyes set in a pale face. She poured a cup of *sake* for him, and he gave her a large tip.

"If you're not too busy, why don't you stay and keep me company."

"I'd be happy to, sir," she replied with a smile.

16

"What's your name?"

"Omoto."

Baian was dressed formally, but he behaved with such easy charm that Omoto immediately found herself attracted to him.

"Is it your first visit here?"

"No, I came once before, about three years ago."

"Oh, really?"

"Things seem to have changed a lot since then."

Omoto did not say anything, but her expression indicated that she agreed. Aside from going to the kitchen to fetch his meal and more *sake*, she stayed with him and made sure that his cup remained full.

The food was not quite as good as it had been during his last visit, and one of the dishes had a small chip in the rim. He pointed this out to Omoto, but she gave a shrug as if to say there was nothing she could do about it.

He stayed for about two hours. By the end of that time Omoto had become quite relaxed with him. When he asked what had happened to cause the many changes in the restaurant, she lowered her voice and said, "It all started when the boss remarried." She had drunk enough *sake* to become a little indiscreet.

"You mean the owner was married before?"

"Yes."

"What happened to his first wife? Did she fall sick?"

"No, she was very healthy. She was an extremely considerate person and looked after the staff well. It was a real pleasure to work for her."

"I see. So that's why the business did so well."

Led on by Baian, Omoto warmed to her story. "Yes. Then one day she suddenly took ill and died."

"Really?"

"Yes, I'll never forget it. She'd gone to pray at the Hachi-man Shrine in Fukagawa when suddenly she collapsed in the middle of the crowd. She never recovered. The constables said it must have been a heart attack."

"I see," Baian muttered in an expressionless tone, as his mind went back to that day.

He was standing in the crowd in front of the shrine. When the owner's wife walked past, he plunged a needle into the hollow at the nape of her neck, without anyone noticing what he was doing. The needle, about four inches long and slightly thicker than the ones he used for acupuncture, traveled up her neck until it reached the brainstem and severed the nerves leading to the spinal cord.

The woman gave a low moan and staggered a few steps before collapsing. By the time the maid who was accompanying her screamed out in alarm, Baian had disappeared into the crowd.

Although the constables examined the body thoroughly, they could not determine the cause of death. In those days medicine was still in its infancy, and the idea of performing an autopsy on the body did not occur to anyone.

Baian could not help the feeling of pride that welled up in him as he listened to Omoto's description of a perfectly executed job. However, if the victim had been as good a person as Omoto described, why would anyone have wanted her killed?

He still could not get over the coincidence of being employed to kill the owner's second wife. He had been in this business for more than ten years now, but he had never heard of anything like it before. He suspected that there was more to this than mere coincidence, and he made up his mind to get to the bottom of it before he fulfilled his contract.

"The present mistress is very difficult to get on with," Omoto said with a sigh. "Staff don't stay here very long, but the master leaves the running of the place entirely in her hands."

When Baian left, he tucked a gold piece in Omoto's sash and whispered in her ear, "Arrange to get some time off tomorrow and come see me at the Izutsu Restaurant in Asakusa. I'll be waiting for you at around ten in the morning."

Without waiting for her reply, he got up and left.

An Afternoon with Omoto

The Izutsu in Asakusa was like a second home to Baian, and he always stayed there when he was in that part of town. It was a very elegant building that stood on the north side of the Hashiba Fudoin Temple. A bamboo grove stood at the back, and there was a beautiful view over the Omoi River of the Masaki Inari Shrine on the opposite bank.

Baian had once saved the life of the Izutsu's owner, Yosuke, staying at his bedside until he had made a full recovery. Ever since, a grateful Yosuke had spared no expense when Baian came to visit the restaurant.

After leaving the Manshichi, Baian took a boat to Asakusa and stayed overnight at the Izutsu.

Next morning at ten, soon after Baian had finished a late breakfast, one of the waitresses showed Omoto to his room. He was staying in an annex in the Izutsu's garden. The bright sun shining through the clear winter air made the translucent paper of the doors glow white. But the doors were all closed, and the room remained in shadow—Baian did not like bright rooms.

Neither spoke until the waitress had brought *sake* and they were left alone again. Baian stared at Omoto's face intently the whole time. She averted her gaze, but he could see the flush of color rise in her cheeks.

"Come and sit down over here. Was it difficult for you to get away?"

"No, I told them that my aunt in Honjo was sick."

"That's good, but tell me, how many times have you killed your aunt in order to meet a man you liked?"

"Do I look like that kind of woman?"

"I was only joking." As he spoke, Baian slid toward her, took her in his arms, and kissed her.

"Your skin's very soft."

"Please, don't…" she whispered breathlessly.

"Don't what?"

She did not answer. Enfolded in Baian's strong arms, her sash was soon undone. Her kimono opened to reveal her full breasts.

"It's good to enjoy yourself now and again, isn't it?" Baian whispered as she lay cradled in his arms, her eyes tightly closed. She nodded slightly and then hugged him to her with surprising strength….

Four hours later, Baian showed Omoto out to the street, and she walked back to Yagenbori, a look of deep content-ment on her face. When she had left, Baian had given her more money.

"It's good to enjoy yourself now and again," he said.

"Yes."

"Let's meet again. If I contact you, will you come and see me?"

"Of course."

"We were made for each other."

"Don't!" she protested. "You're embarrassing me."

During brief pauses in their frenzied love-making, Baian

managed to question her about the Manshichi without her realizing it. He listened attentively to everything she said about herself, and she felt flattered. She was not particularly pretty, but she had a shapely figure, and it was a pleasure for Baian to employ her for his own ends.

Baian stayed at the Izutsu for two more days before returning home to Shinagawadai. That night it started to snow, and when he awoke the next morning, he found that it had settled quite deeply.

He stayed in bed until Oseki finished the cleaning shortly after noon. He got up and put a potful of thin broth on the brazier in the living room, added some white radish and fried tofu, and left it to simmer. Afterwards, while he was eating, he got out a flask of *sake* and settled down to think over everything he had learned so far.

Omoto had told him that the present mistress of the Manshichi, Omino, was twenty-five years old, and that she had once worked as a prostitute in a teahouse in Honjo. Her beauty was so widely acclaimed that she had even become an artist's model. Five years earlier Zenshiro, the owner of the Manshichi, had become so infatuated with her that he used to visit her at the teahouse every day.

"That was before I started to work at the restaurant," Omoto said, "but I heard that he was the talk of the neighborhood. He had been a very quiet man before that; he did not drink or smoke, and it was rumored that he had known no woman other than his wife.

"Be that as it may, he lost all sense of reason after he met Omino and spent huge amounts of money on her. However, his wife did not seem to worry about his infidelity, and she worked as hard as ever to ensure the success of the business. She never had an unkind word for him, and when she was asked about the affair, she merely replied: 'He's a good

man. This is only a temporary thing. He'll soon get over it.'
I started work at Manshichi about three months before she
died."

Omino moved into the Manshichi less than a year after
the mistress's death and virtually forced Zenshiro to marry
her. Although his relatives could not believe that he was serious and did everything they could to stop him, he wouldn't
listen, and the couple were married in the restaurant. Zenshiro's daughter by his first wife could not bear to live in
the same house as her stepmother and had gone to stay
with her mother's relatives.

Once she had managed to take over the business, Omino forced everyone she did not like to leave. This caused a
lot of ill will, and at one point the staff dropped to one-
third its original size. In order to make up the numbers she
had employed new cooks and waitresses and became the
real boss at last.

Even though she had been able to sell herself to men at
the teahouse, she did not have what it took to run a high-
class restaurant. All the people she hired were hardworking
when she was watching, but as soon as she turned her back,
they did their best to swindle her. She trusted the people
who flattered her, but the cooks bought low-quality food,
pocketing the money they saved, while the waitresses did
not bother to do the cleaning properly, preferring instead
to sit around chatting or go out to the shops. It was only
natural that business should begin to suffer.

Zenshiro stayed in bed most of the day, getting up only
in the evening to drink with Omino. He had become pale
and lost a lot of weight. All he thought about was his new
wife, and everybody agreed that unless he changed his ways
he did not have much longer to live.

After finishing the stew, Baian picked up a brush and

drew a plan of the Manshichi. He had visited the restaurant again to talk with Omoto, and along with the information he managed to obtain from her and his own observations, he had a good idea of the layout of the building.

The one thing he had not been able to discover was who had hired him to kill Zenshiro's first wife.

The Bargain

Baian stayed home even after the snow melted, venturing out only to visit Kinzo and his other patients.

He did not hear any more from Ichibei. He obviously trusted Baian, and anyway there was no hurry for him to finish the job.

A few days later he was sitting in his house when a man named Gomyo paid him a call. Gomyo was about seventy years old, and there very few people in the underworld who had not heard of him. It was he who three years earlier, at the request of Kahei, the Honjo district boss, had come to ask Baian to kill Zenshiro's first wife.

"How have you been doing?" he asked Baian as he came into the room.

"I've been fine and I must say you look very fit, too. What can I do for you today?"

"I came to see if you could deal with someone for me."

The man he wanted killed was a high official called Ito. It would not be an easy job. Samurai lived together in large mansions, and it was very difficult to get close to them.

"There is no hurry to finish the job, as long as you do it within about…say…one year."

He put seventy-five gold pieces on the table as the advance. This meant that whoever wanted Ito dead had been willing to pay Kahei three hundred gold pieces for the job.

There were all kinds of feuds among the upper echelons of the samurai class, and they often resorted to violence to resolve them, so there was no telling who might have paid the money to have the job done.

"I hope you'll agree to do it. It's a bit tricky and I don't know who else to turn to."

"Really?"

"Yes, nobody else could manage a job like this."

Baian thought it over for a few minutes, then he said, "I'll do it on one condition."

"Which is?"

"I want to know who paid to have the wife of the owner of the Manshichi killed three years ago."

Gomyo's eyes flashed in surprise.

"Don't ask me why I want to know," Baian went on. "It's nothing special, I'm just interested."

Gomyo remained silent and looked searchingly at the assassin.

"I know that I'm breaking the rules by asking you, and if you don't want to tell me, fine—but you'll have to find somebody else to do this job," Baian said coolly.

"It doesn't look as though I have any choice," Gomyo said with a sigh. "I know that I can trust you not to do anything stupid, but the gods help me if the boss finds out that I told you."

"Thank you."

"It was his present wife, Omino."

"What?"

"Yes. We didn't want to take the job on to begin with, but the request came from the boss of the Shiba area, so we couldn't refuse." The boss of the Shiba area was the most powerful man in the Edo underworld. "Omino was a prostitute then," Gomyo continued, "and working for a pimp called Shinsuke. He's a really bad type, and it was probably him who arranged for her to get the contract taken out. I'm sorry, I shouldn't be telling you all this—but will you take the job now?"

Baian did not reply, he just picked up the coins in silence.

"Thank you. The boss will be pleased to hear it. I can assure you that this job will not leave a bad taste in your mouth like the Manshichi one. Shinsuke is a bad one, even though I say so myself."

"You've become very talkative in your old age."

"That's true, but I know I can trust you."

"I've already forgotten what you told me."

"Well, if you can get started on the Ito job, then."

"Soon. Give my regards to the boss."

"Yes, I'll do that."

The following day Baian left his house to visit the Manshichi. Omoto rushed out to greet him and showed him to a private room.

"The mistress would like to meet you," she said as she brought his *sake*.

Baian thought for a moment.

"All right."

This would be the first time that he would see the woman who had paid him to kill the owner's previous wife, and whom he would now kill.

"Excuse me," Omino said and swept into the room. Baian's face froze.

"What's wrong?" Omino asked.

"Oh, I beg your pardon," Baian apologized. "I was just startled by your beauty."

"Oh, you shouldn't flatter me like that," Omino said,

moving closer to him and pouring him a drink. Her shoulder brushed against his chest. Even through her kimono he could feel the softness of her body. He swallowed hard.

Omino was confident of her charms and settled down to make him feel at home. She realized that he was one of her few regular customers, and with the way business was going for her recently, she could not afford to lose him. But after only a short while, Baian stood up.

"I'm afraid I will have to be going now," he said.

"What, already? Can't you stay with me a little longer?"

She did not sound at all like the proprietress of a first-class restaurant. She had worked as a prostitute for so long that she did not know any other way to entertain her male customers.

Omoto showed Baian out to the front door.

"I was going to ask you to come to meet me at the Izutsu tomorrow, but I've just remembered some urgent business. I will definitely get in touch with you soon, though, don't worry."

"I'll be waiting," Omoto whispered ardently.

Once he reached the street, he stopped a palanquin and told the bearers to take him to Shinagawadai.

When Oseki arrived to do the cleaning in the morning, she was surprised to find Baian still in bed.

"I had to put off my business for a little longer," he said lazily.

That night he prepared his acupuncture needles. There were dozens of them. He cleaned each one with alcohol and sharpened the thicker ones that were used for drawing blood. There were three particularly sturdy needles, each about four inches long, over which he took special trouble —his assassin's needles.

A Nighttime Visitor

The days had been growing gradually warmer since the night it had snowed.

Five days after Gomyo's visit Baian went out, telling Oseki that he would be back late.

In the middle of the night he slipped into the Manshichi unnoticed. He climbed onto the roof of a neighboring house and crept from rooftop to rooftop until he came to the Manshichi's inner garden. His movements were slow, as usual, but he moved with an easy grace, passing through the night without making a sound to betray himself. If any of his neighbors had seen him now, as he moved wraithlike over the roofs, they would not have believed their eyes.

He slipped under the building from the garden and crawled until he was directly below the floor of one of the storerooms. Using a dagger, he pried one of the floorboards loose and climbed in. The building was silent, and as he crept down the hall he could hear the breathing of the servants in the rooms he passed. He was wearing a dark kimono with the hem tucked up into his sash at the back. He had dark blue trousers and *tabi* socks, and his face was masked with a piece of dark-colored cloth. His straw sandals were tucked into his sash so that he made no sound as he walked.

He came to the master bedroom, from which he could hear someone's ragged breathing. Sliding the door open a fraction, he peered in and saw Zenshiro sleeping by himself. The room smelled of medicine.

He closed the door again and continued around the corner to Omino's room. He crept into the room adjoining the bedroom and opened the door silently. She was lying in bed, her arms and legs entangled with those of a man in his mid-thirties. Their clothes lay scattered around the room.

Baian guessed that the man must be Omino's former pimp, Shinsuke. He slipped into the room and squatted at the end of the bed for a moment, never taking his eyes off their faces. There was a tray with a flask of water and a cup by Omino's pillow. Crawling over to it, he moved the cup away, then poured the water onto the tray.

He took a sheet of thick paper from his kimono and spread it in the water to soak. He then slipped a large leather ring onto the finger of his right hand. Moving with fluid grace, he reached inside his kimono with his left hand, took out an assassin's needle, and placed it between his lips.

Next he spread the wet paper on the tatami mat next to the bed and sat looking down at Omino's face in the dim light of the lantern that illuminated the room.

Her hair was in disarray, and her mouth hung half open, giving him a view of her fashionably blackened teeth. Her left shoulder was exposed, and he could see numerous bite marks on her body, which spoke of the frenzy of the couple's lovemaking earlier that night.

As he looked at her, an indescribable look of anger and regret played briefly over his features.

Suddenly he moved. With almost superhuman speed he picked up the sheet of paper with his left hand and plastered it over her face. He pulled the bedding down to her waist and grasped the needle he had been holding in his mouth with his right hand. Omino's eyes flew open in shock at finding the paper on her face, but before she could call out, Baian plunged the needle straight into her heart. Her body twitched twice, and then she lay still. The man lying next to her continued to snore.

The room smelled of *sake* and sex. Baian grimaced in disgust and covered her body with the bedclothes again before backing slowly out of the room.

Two hours later he was sitting in his own bedroom, drinking a cup of *sake*. It was not long before dawn. Crawling into bed, he was soon fast asleep, a relaxed look on his face.

Baian's Story

Spring arrived, and with it the warm weather. The cherry trees on the banks of the Okawa River were in full bloom. The riverside restaurants and teahouses were packed with people who had come to see the cherry blossoms. This was their busiest season. The Izutsu was no exception and was filled with customers, but while the main building was very noisy, the annex seemed almost deserted. Baian had come with Hikojiro, who lived nearby.

Hikojiro looked over fifty, but Baian had no idea how old he really was; all he knew was that Hikojiro was older than he was. Most people thought that he made toothpicks for a living, but his real trade was murder. Baian had taught him how to use an assassin's needle for the job. They had worked together several times in the past and each admired the other's skill. There were no secrets between them, and that was why they were able to relax and drink together in this way.

"You mean that it was you who killed the mistress of the Manshichi?" Hikojiro exclaimed in surprise after Baian had told him the whole story. "The minute I heard about it, I said to myself, this is a professional job."

Omino's body had been discovered the following morning by a maid who had gone to wake her. There was no sign of Omino's lover, who must have fled as soon as he realized

what had happened. As Baian guessed, the man was Shinsuke, but it had done him no good to flee, for he had soon
been caught.

"I slept with her, but I didn't kill her," Shinsuke said.
"When I saw she was dead, I panicked and ran away, but
that was all." The more he tried to explain, the worse it became. Judging from the dried blood on Omino's breast,
the constables realized that she had been stabbed with a
needle-like instrument.

"They say that he's going to be executed soon," Hikojiro
said.

"He deserves it."

"The owner of the restaurant was already sick, and the
shock of hearing of his wife's death proved too much for
him. He died soon after."

"I see."

"His daughter had been staying with relatives, but she
came back to take over the business. The family is going to
find her a good husband and then help them get the Manshichi on its feet again. It's the talk of the area. But it's not
often that you hear of something like this."

"What?"

"One man killing both wives of the same man."

"That's true," Baian said putting down his cup. "You
know, I'm pretty sure the second wife was my sister."

"What?!" Hikojiro could not hide his surprise. "Are you
serious?"

"Yes, she was the spitting image of my mother. No two
people could resemble each other that much without being
related."

"Did you realize it before you killed her?"

"Yes."

A maid entered the room with another flask of *sake* and

a plate of fish sautéed with bamboo shoots. They fell silent, listening to a bird singing in the garden.

"The birds are busy making their nests," Baian said after the maid left.

Hikojiro drank his *sake*, glancing over at Baian every now and again. Baian could guess what he was thinking, so he decided to explain.

"I've never told you much about myself, have I? I was born at Fujieda, where my father had a business making wooden buckets."

"What about your sister?"

"She must have been around four or five years old when my father died. She always seemed to have a cold and spent most of her time crying." He shook his head. "I never dreamed that she would turn into such a formidable woman."

"Did she have the same name?"

"No, in those days she was called something else, but that doesn't mean anything—women change their names all the time."

"But you are sure that the mistress of the Manshichi was really your sister?"

"Yes, without a doubt," Baian said coldly. "The day my father died, my mother cried her eyes out over his body, but the next morning she ran off with another man, leaving me to fend for myself. She took my sister with her, though."

"I see."

"Women are terrible creatures. Their tears mean nothing. My father's death must have seemed like the answer to a prayer for my mother, but she still made a show of crying over his body." He spoke with unusual vehemence.

"I was left with nothing, and I don't know what would have happened to me if I hadn't met Etsudo, a doctor who

31

happened to be passing through on his way home to Kyoto from Edo. He took me back with him and treated me like his son. He taught me everything I know about acupuncture."

"So that's how you became a doctor."

"Yes, but things didn't go quite as I had planned." He gave a bitter laugh. "He died when I was twenty-five, and shortly after that I killed for the first time."

"A woman?"

"Yes. She was just like my mother and sister. I don't mean the way she looked, but in the way she acted."

The maid came in again with more *sake* and two bowls of soup on a tray. The soup, made from fish stock, was the speciality of the restaurant. A single orchid bloom floated on the surface of each serving.

"I'll never kill another woman for money."

"I can understand that."

"Don't get me wrong, it has nothing to do with my having killed my sister."

"Eh?"

"Now that I know more about the circumstances, I regret having killed the first mistress of the Manshichi."

"But that was the fault of that bastard, Kahei."

"Yes, and that's why I never want to work for him again," he said, looking rather disgruntled. "There's one more job that I have to do for him, however."

"Have you already accepted it?"

"Yes, for one hundred fifty gold pieces."

"It must be a tough one then."

"Yes, a samurai. I've got a year to do it, though."

"Sounds interesting."

"Yes, but I first have some unfinished business to take care of, and then I thoughts I'd go for a holiday in Atami before I start preparing for the Ito job."

"By the way..."

"What?"

"What did you say was the name of the maid at Man-shichi who you got friendly with?"

"Omoto."

"Have you seen her again?"

"No, I haven't," he replied, his eyes softening. "She was a kind woman, and I want to remember her that way."

"What do you mean?"

"There is no telling when she might turn out like my mother or sister—women are all the same at heart, you know."

THE UNCERTAIN ASSASSIN

It was a fine spring afternoon in the garden of the Tachibanaya Inn. On the other side of the hedge, a menacing gloom enveloped the cedar grove of the Kishimojin Shrine, and the air was filled with the mournful dirge of pilgrims at prayer.

The Tachibanaya's imposing main gate announced that it was more than just an ordinary suburban inn. An elder of the Kii clan had chosen it as his official residence whenever he visited Japan's eastern capital of Edo.

A small cottage stood on the grounds of the inn. Although with its thatched roof it looked like a poor farmer's house, a closer inspection revealed that no expense had been spared in its construction. It epitomized the austere taste of the warrior class, which scorned ostentatious displays of wealth.

A well-dressed samurai in his forties was just then being led down the long covered walkway that linked the cottage to the main building of the inn. From the way the inn's owner, Chubei, had greeted the guest in person at the main entrance, it was clear that the samurai was a man of some importance. His name was Kawamura, and he was a senior official of the Kii clan. Strangely, he had come without his attendants, traveling incognito in a commoner's palanquin.

"I know I don't have to tell you," Kawamura said as Chubei poured some *sake* into a porcelain cup, "that this visit must be kept secret."

"I quite understand, your excellency," Chubei said.

"I'm expecting a man by the name of Iseya in an hour's time. He'll be accompanied by a woman."

"I'll show them in as soon as they arrive, excellency."

The two men chatted for a little while, and then Chubei made his way back to the inn. Kawamura sat drinking by himself, looking out at the garden through the open sliding doors. Kawamura's keen eyes followed a small white butterfly as it flitted from flower to flower, and a faint smile played across his lips. Then he set his cup down and rose to go to the cottage's toilet.

On returning to his room, he immediately noticed that something was wrong. The translucent paper doors opening on the garden had been closed, but when he looked around, no one else was in the room.

Who could have closed them? Kawamura asked himself. And why? He had not ordered them closed, and on such a fine day there was no need to do so, until his guests arrived.

He walked over to open them, but as he did so he sensed someone's presence behind him. He spun around and saw a giant of a man bearing down on him without a sound.

Kawamura tried to call for help, but the giant's hand strangled the cry in his throat. A metallic object flashing in the assassin's free hand was the last thing Kawamura ever saw. The next moment he was dead.

Fujieda Baian let the lifeless body slide to the floor. He

leaned over the corpse to retrieve the four-inch needle he had imbedded in Kawamura's brain through his ear, wiped it clean, and put it back into his kimono.

Baian checked the room quickly, then opened the doors to the garden a fraction to make sure the way was clear. He was about to step out when he heard a sound behind him. Startled, Baian turned round just in time to see a young woman climbing out of a low cupboard set into an alcove. She ran out of the room screaming, waving her arms in front of her as if she were swimming.

There was no time for him to deal with her. No, that was not true, he might have managed it, but he was too stunned to move. He had been hired to kill only Kawamura, but once an assassin was seen he had no choice but to kill any witnesses.

Baian cursed under his breath. He could not afford to remain any longer. Running across the garden, he leaped over the hedge and vanished among the trees.

Clam Stew

The next evening Baian's friend Hikojiro visited him at his home in Shinagawa, a southern suburb of Edo.

When Hikojiro arrived, Baian was taking a bath, his gigantic frame squeezed into a small wooden tub.

"Good evening," Hikojiro called out, entering the house.

The sound of splashing stopped, but there was no reply. Hikojiro walked through to the kitchen and found a basket of clams and another of tofu, which Oseki must have left out for his evening meal.

"Hey, Baian, it looks as if you've been busy today."

"Yes, I've got a lot of patients at the moment, and they don't leave me much free time," Baian replied from the bathroom.

"Shall I heat up some *sake*?" Hikojiro asked.

"Yes. But wouldn't you like to have a bath first? I'm almost done."

"Nah, I'll have one before I go to bed."

The day before, Baian had gone to Hikojiro's house near Asakusa and explained that a woman had seen him on a job. Hikojiro had quickly grasped what Baian wanted of him.

"Don't worry," he had told him. "I'll do a bit of investigating and see what I can turn up."

While Baian finished his bath, Hikojiro lit the brazier and put a stewing pot filled with stock on the fire. He added water, salt, *sake*, and soy sauce for flavoring. He then set the clams, tofu, and sliced leeks to one side, ready for stewing, and proceeded to warm the *sake*.

It started to rain.

"It's kind of cold out today," Hikojiro remarked.

"You arrived just in time."

"You can say that again. I think I'm getting a bit of a cold, and the last thing I want is to get caught in the rain."

"Don't worry, I'll give you some acupuncture later—that ought to take care of it."

"Thanks a lot. I'm sure your needles will make me feel like a new man."

"Acupuncture should be performed while you're still healthy, not after you fall sick. It's the same with any medical treatment, but laymen don't understand that. They wait until they're sick, and then start clamoring for drugs and treatment when it's already too late."

"The *sake*'s ready," Hikojiro said, pouring from the heated flask into Baian's cup. Baian took a sip, then poured a cupful for Hikojiro.

"What did you manage to find out?"

"The woman who saw you is called Otoki. She's one of

40

the hostesses working at the inn."

"I see," Baian said pensively.

"I stayed the night at a teahouse next to the Kishimojin Shrine, and I got lucky—a girl I met there told me she helped out at the Tachibanaya when they got busy."

"And?"

"Well, needless to say, all hell broke loose after you left. There were constables in and out of the place, not to mention the people from the Kii clan. Anyway," Hikojiro went on, "Otoki told the constables that she was on her way to the cottage when she heard someone cry out. She went to investigate and saw Kawamura, one of their best customers, lying on the floor. She called his name several times, but when she realized he was dead, she got frightened and screamed."

The girl in the teahouse had gotten the story straight from one of the hostesses at the Tachibanaya, Hikojiro explained.

"Otoki didn't say anything about having seen you. Are you sure you don't know her?"

"I only caught a glimpse of her, but I don't remember ever having met her before. Did you see her?" Baian asked.

"No, the Tachibanaya was closed, as you'd expect. After all, the man you killed was one of the most powerful retainers of the Kii clan."

Baian nodded.

"I guess he must've been a pretty evil man," Hikojiro mused.

Baian nodded again.

"The stew's done," Hikojiro said, changing the subject.

Baian's chopsticks reached for the pot but then hesitated, hovering over a plate of Oseki's homemade pickled eggplants, before they returned to the pot once more to pick up a piece of tofu.

"It's unlike you not to be able to make up your mind like that. Anyway, when are you going to kill her?"

Baian gave a weak smile and popped the tofu into his mouth.

"I may not kill her."

"What do you mean?" Hikojiro exclaimed in surprise. "Anyone who sees an assassin on a job has to die. That's the rule we work by, and you know it as well as I do. This isn't like you at all."

"I know you're right, but still…"

Hikojiro's Choice

Hikojiro stayed at Baian's house for three days and realized that Baian had not exaggerated his busy schedule. Every morning, after a light breakfast, Baian would hurry out and make house calls until the afternoon. When he returned home, more patients were waiting to see him. Hikojiro found himself being roped in as an assistant.

"I never knew what your practice was like," Hikojiro said.

Each evening after the last patient had left, Baian would be so drenched with sweat that he had to take a bath. This was not due to the heat, however, but to the enormous physical strain produced by the precision needed to perform acupuncture. When he sat down to dinner after his bath, Baian's huge body seemed shrunken. Dark shadows circled his eyes.

"Why do I have to have so many patients all of a sudden?" he complained, sitting at the table with Hikojiro.

Hikojiro had stayed at Baian's house, waiting for him to decide what he would do about Otoki. But, despite Hikojiro's patience, Baian had avoided the subject.

One evening Hikojiro could wait no longer. "I'm going home tomorrow," he said.

"I made up my mind today," Baian said.

"So that explains it."

"Explains what?"

"All the time I've been here you've been picking at your food, unable to decide what you wanted to eat. Today you had no problem."

"Really? I hadn't noticed."

"So what's your decision?"

"I'm not going to do it."

"What?"

"I am not going to kill Otoki."

Hikojiro was silent.

"I don't get it. She saw me, but she didn't tell the authorities. Anyway, I've decided that I'm not going to kill her, and if that means that I'm caught and punished, then so be it. It's about time my luck ran out. I allowed myself to be seen on a job, so I'm no longer fit to be a hired assassin."

Hikojiro raised his *sake* cup in silence. Baian too said nothing more.

The next morning Hikojiro took his leave.

"I'll come by again soon," he said brightly.

Baian just nodded silently and watched him go.

The previous night, while listening to Baian's snores, Hikojiro had made up his mind to act. If Baian isn't going to do anything about that woman, he thought, then I'll do it for him.

He did not know why Otoki had decided to protect Baian, but he did know that women were not to be trusted. Even if she did not tell the authorities, she might gossip about it with someone who would. Women, as far as Hikojiro was concerned, talked first and thought later. If she were dead, there would be nothing more to worry about.

When he got home he took out his favorite weapon: a

blowpipe. Then he changed his mind, opting instead for a short-bladed dagger. He also prepared the assassin's needle Baian had taught him to use.

If it comes down to choosing between this woman and Baian, Hikojiro thought as he sharpened his dagger, I know what my choice will be.

On his way home that night, he had stopped at the barber to have his hair done. The next morning he shaved carefully and put on a neatly pressed kimono. He now looked every inch the wealthy merchant.

He set out for Zoshigaya, arriving around noon. He walked past the teahouse where he had stayed a few days before and went straight to the Tachibanaya.

"I'd like to have some lunch," he said to the middle-aged hostess who greeted him at the door.

"Please come this way, sir," she said, leading him into the building.

Hikojiro was surprised to see how crowded the place was in spite of the recent murder, but then he realized that most of the customers were probably out-of-town pilgrims who were on their way to the neighboring shrine and would be quite ignorant of the affair.

The hostess took him to a pretty little private room overlooking the garden. She poured a cup of *sake* for him, and he took a sip.

"Does a hostess called Otoki still work here?" he asked casually.

"Why, yes, sir. Do you know her?"

"When I came here last time with my family she served us. She was very good with the children. If she's here…"

"I'm sorry, sir, but she's away."

Hikojiro had slipped the hostess a good tip, so she was more than happy to gossip.

"She got word this morning that her brother, Sotaro, was sick, and she asked for time off to look after him. I expect she'll be back in a couple of days." Then she confided, "He's her only living relative, you see."

"Is that so?" Hikojiro said, encouraging her to go on.

"He works for the Kagiya wallet shop in Akasaka. He's just an apprentice of twenty, but he plans to have his own shop one day."

Realizing that he could do nothing more right then, Hikojiro ate his meal and ordered a palanquin.

As soon as the hostess was out of earshot he said to the bearers, "Take me to Akasaka as fast as you can."

Kinzo's Advice

"It sounds bad, I know," Kinzo the clogmaker said. "But don't worry, I know a doctor who'll have him on his feet again in no time."

Kinzo was sitting in the kitchen of the Kagiya wallet shop, drinking the tea that the servant girl Omitsu had just served him.

The Kagiya was famous for its leather tobacco pouches. Risuke, the owner, had much of his stock made to order in Kyoto, where Japan's best craftsmen lived. He counted many provincial lords and courtiers among his customers. The shop itself was small, but the business had been in Risuke's family for five generations, and he was well-known local figure.

Kinzo's wife, Odai, had worked at the Kagiya before getting married, so both she and Kinzo were on friendly terms with Risuke. The owner of the Kagiya was extremely fond of a kind of rice cracker made near Kinzo's home in Shinagawa, so whenever the clogmaker had to go to Akasaka he would bring Risuke some crackers.

That day, Kinzo had gone to the kitchen to be reimbursed for the crackers and to receive a small tip for his trouble, which was the real reason he was willing to make the trip.

"Is that you, Kinzo?" Risuke's wife said, coming into the kitchen. "I'm afraid the master's out, but he'll be delighted when he sees the crackers."

"It's nothing, ma'am, it's the least we can do."

"How are Odai and the children?"

"They're fine, ma'am. But I hear that poor Sotaro is not well."

"Yes, poor boy, he's burning up with fever. He's lost his appetite, and yesterday he threw up several times. Today, he keeps blacking out. The master was so worried that he sent for the doctor, but it didn't make any difference at all."

"That sounds just like something I had a while back."

"You look fine now."

"Yes, thanks to a doctor who lives in the neighborhood. I was just telling Omitsu about him. His name is Fujieda Baian; he's an acupuncturist—though to tell the truth, he looks more like a sumo wrestler."

Risuke's wife thought for a moment, then said, "Sotaro was so bad yesterday that I sent for his sister. Would this doctor of yours be willing to come and see him here?"

"Of course, leave it to me," Kinzo replied, slapping his chest confidently.

"Wait here a moment," she said, going inside.

Kinzo was telling jokes to the servant girl when Risuke's wife came back with a pretty young woman in her mid-twenties.

"Kinzo, this is Otoki, Sotaro's sister. I've told her about Dr. Baian and she'd very much like him to look at Sotaro, if he'll come."

46

❖ ❖ ❖

Hikojiro stepped off the palanquin a little way from the Kagiya.

So what now? he asked himself. I don't even know what Otoki looks like.

He spotted a noodle restaurant on the opposite side of the road, where he could sit and have a drink while keeping watch on the shop. But just as he was crossing the road, a man and woman came through the Kagiya's side door.

The minute Hikojiro saw the woman he was certain she was Otoki. She was short and had a trim figure, but the cut of her kimono and her hairstyle could not be those of the daughter of a respectable tradesman's family.

Although her face was pale and she had dark rings under her eyes, Hikojiro could tell that Otoki was the kind of woman that men found irresistible. Working as a hostess at a high-class inn and entertaining male guests every day, she had learned to make her every movement exude sensuality. The man with her was obviously overpowered by her charms.

Hikojiro had no way of knowing that Kinzo was Baian's neighbor and regular patient. He decided to follow the couple.

It was three o'clock on a spring afternoon, and the sun was still high. Hikojiro cursed as he followed them up Ushinakizaka. Since that man is with her I can't do a thing until it gets dark, he thought.

The pair crossed the Azabu Bridge and walked through the temple district of Mita until they reached the Nihon-Enoki road.

It looks as if...no, it couldn't be. Hikojiro began to worry. Every step they took led them closer to Baian's house. Was the man with her a constable?

The two walked through Shiroganedai, and Hikojiro could no longer doubt their destination. The right-hand side of the road they took was bordered by the woodland of the Kijinomiya Shrine. Baian's house was only minutes away.

Otoki's Story

Otoki's father had been a pipemaker. Her mother died when Sotaro was six years old, and Otoki had raised him in her place. Although their father did not drink or have anything to do with other women, his one vice was gambling. He spent most of his free time going from one gambling den to another, but he always made sure that his children had enough to eat.

A skilled craftsman, he turned out wares for a large shop in the center of town, but he also made special orders for a few private customers, including Risuke, the Kagiya's owner. That was why, when Sotaro reached the age of thirteen, Risuke offered to take him on as an apprentice. Otoki was eighteen at the time.

"It's your turn next," Otoki's father told her one evening. "You've had a tough life with me but I'm going to see to it that you make a good marriage and never want for anything ever again."

Sadly, he died suddenly before he could keep his promise, leaving Otoki on her own. She had few relatives, and none was willing to take her in.

The new year came. Otoki turned nineteen, but still she had nowhere to go. The master of the Kagiya offered to take her in, but she felt that it would not be fair to Sotaro if she worked in the same house, so she declined.

Then one day, Chubei, the owner of the Tachibanaya,

came to order a new pipe. Otoki's father did not like working for him because he was a fussy customer, but he paid well so he could not turn him down.

Otoki had met Chubei several times previously, but in the past year she had turned from a gangling adolescent into a beautiful young woman. Chubei could hardly keep his eyes off her. After hearing her story, he offered her a job as a hostess at the inn.

The Tachibanaya hostesses were not paid a wage, but they were allowed to keep their tips, so the harder they worked, the more they earned. Otoki thought it over for three days and then moved into the Tachibanaya.

Six years had passed since then, and they had been hard years for her. She was too old at twenty-five to think of marriage. During her years as a hostess she had had affairs with several of the customers, which accounted for a large proportion of her earnings.

She decided to save her money to help Sotaro set up a shop of his own. This was all that mattered to her now, and she worked harder than ever to save as much money as possible, dreaming of the time when she would live with him and help with his business. Sotaro had always seemed more like a son than a brother to her, and now she realized that he was the only son she would ever have.

House Call

To say that Hikojiro was amazed when Kinzo and Otoki entered Baian's house would be an understatement.

What on earth is going on? he asked himself as he hurried around to the back of the house. At least the man did not appear to be a constable. If he had been he would have told Otoki to wait outside while he went in, truncheon in hand. The man had walked in calmly with the woman, as if he were visiting an old friend. In any case, Kinzo just did not look like the kind of man who would be chosen to uphold the peace.

Baian's maid, Oseki, came out of the house and found Hikojiro loitering in the yard.

"What are you doing out here?" she asked.

"Oh, er…nothing. Is Baian at home?"

"Yes, he'd just seen his last patient when the clogmaker turned up with some woman to see him. The doctor said he wouldn't be needing me any more so I'm going home."

"Did you say he was a clogmaker?"

"Yes, besides being a drunk, too."

Hikojiro heaved a sigh of relief and stepped past Oseki into the house. He crouched down in the kitchen to listen to what was going on in the next room, but all he could hear was Kinzo explaining to Baian why he had brought Otoki to see him.

"I would appreciate your help," Otoki added when Kinzo had finished. Hikojiro noticed that her voice trembled slightly.

"You may leave now, Kinzo," Baian said. "I will go with this lady to look at her brother."

"Really?" Kinzo replied. "Your brother will be all right now, you'll see."

"Well…that's…" Otoki stuttered, the fear now evident in her voice.

It looks as if neither Baian nor the woman were prepared for this meeting, Hikojiro realized, allowing himself to relax a little.

"Don't worry, don't worry, everything will be fine now," Kinzo said blithely, not understanding why Otoki was so upset. "Well, I'll be off then."

Kinzo sauntered out of the house without giving Otoki a

chance to stop him. His departure was followed by a long pause.

"Is that you hiding in the kitchen, Hikojiro?" Baian called out.

"Yes," Hikojiro replied, but he stayed in his hiding place.

"I'm going out with this lady to look at her brother. Will you look after the house for me?"

"Of course."

Hikojiro heard Baian get up, and the woman gave a low moan.

"Don't be afraid," Baian said. "I'm not going to hurt you. You spared my life, so the least I can do is cure your brother, if it's humanly possible."

Baian collected his needles, then headed for the door, the woman following unsteadily.

Hikojiro hurried out the back of the house just in time to see Otoki's pale face as she walked by. She was completely intimidated by Baian's size and was helpless to resist him.

Dusk was approaching, and the sound of children playing could be heard from the shrine woods.

So everything has turned out fine in the end, Hikojiro mused. She's like a rabbit transfixed by a snake. He had no doubt that Baian was about to kill Otoki. Now that's what I call jumping from the frying pan into the fire, he chuckled to himself. I wonder where he'll deal with her. It probably won't take long, so I better get the *sake* ready.

Hikojiro heated the bath water, then went into the kitchen and started to peel vegetables for dinner, whistling as he worked.

Baian, however, did not return until very late that night. Hikojiro was so worried about him that he walked along the road in the direction of Shiroganedai several times to check for any sign of him. Finally Baian's huge shadow appeared in the doorway.

"Where have you been?" Hikojiro asked him instead of greeting him. "Is it all over now?"

"Yes, it's finished."

"That's a relief. She should be thankful it was you who killed her. At least she'll have died without pain."

"What are you talking about?"

"Otoki."

"I haven't done anything to her."

"But—"

"I went to treat her brother, and I think he's going to be all right."

Baian smiled and Hikojiro looked at him in amazement.

"Are you sure that was the right thing to do?"

"Yes, I've made my decision. If she goes to the authorities, and I'm arrested and executed, then so be it."

"But that's crazy!"

"We all have to die sometime, you said so yourself."

Hikojiro suddenly realized that there was something different about Baian that evening. His enormous body seemed filled with dignity. Hikojiro said no more.

"Is the *sake* ready?" Baian asked. "I'll tell you about Otoki over a drink."

The Silent Hostess

Otoki refused to tell the authorities what she had witnessed that day because she thought Kawamura deserved to die. When she saw Baian slip into the room from the garden like a cat and kill Kawamura, she was too terrified to call out. But as he was preparing to escape, she could not control herself any longer. She had run away because she was terrified for her own life, not because of what she had seen Baian do to Kawamura.

"I thought that you were going to kill me, too," she told Baian.

It was not until Otoki reached the inn and raised the alarm that she realized that she was glad that Kawamura was dead. It was almost as if the murderer had killed him for her. And not just for her but for all the women who had suffered at his hands. It was then that she decided that under no circumstances would she say anything to put Baian in jeopardy.

She had been forced to sleep with Kawamura three times. He had preyed on all the younger hostesses of the inn. None of them slept with him willingly, but when Chubei ordered them to, they had no choice.

Because the hostesses lived off tips, when they were offered a large enough sum most of them agreed to sleep with a customer. But they were not common prostitutes, and they retained the right to say no.

Kawamura was different; he never paid. But still Chubei insisted that they sleep with him. The Kii clan's patronage lent the inn prestige that Chubei was unwilling to risk losing. Kawamura was one of the most powerful retainers of the clan, and he had come not only for the company of the hostesses but also to hold secret meetings with Chubei and other members of the clan.

"I don't know what Kawamura talked about with his guests," Otoki said. "But whatever it was, I'm sure it involved sex and money. He used his position to line his own pockets." She dropped her eyes. "Of course, Chubei is different," she added in a low voice, but to Baian it sounded as if she really meant to say, "Of course, Chubei is as bad as all the rest."

The hostesses hated going with Kawamura, but there was nothing they could do about it.

"We couldn't refuse him, but that bastard, I mean Kawamura, did terrible things...he was like a beast."

"But what were you doing in the cupboard that day in the first place? Were you going to see him afterward?"

"No, it was nothing like that. I was there on Chubei's orders."

"You mean Chubei had told you to hide in the cupboard?"

"Yes, he told me to eavesdrop on Kawamura's conversation."

Baian closed his eyes for a moment.

"Do you sleep with Chubei?" he asked quietly.

"No, never," Otoki answered firmly. "That day, Kawamura had planned to meet a man called Iseya. He said that he would be bringing a woman with him," she added.

"A woman?"

"Yes."

"Was it the first time he had come to the Tachibanaya?"

"I don't know, but none of the other girls seem to have heard of him."

"And did this Iseya turn up after I killed Kawamura?"

Otoki's voice faded into a mumble, and she shook her head.

"So he didn't come."

There was a tremendous commotion after Otoki raised the alarm. It was more than likely that Iseya, realizing something was wrong, had left as soon as the constables had arrived. But Baian suspected that Hanemon, the underworld chief who had hired him to do the job, had used Iseya's visit to lure Kawamura to the restaurant that day.

"You'd better stay here and look after Sotaro. Don't leave the house, whatever happens," Baian warned her.

Otoki's eyes filled with fear again.

"You've hidden in that cupboard to spy on customers before, haven't you? Be honest."

Otoki lowered her eyes.

"He trusted you not to talk, am I right?"

Again, she did not answer.

"I suppose he probably paid you well for what you did."

"Tell me," Otoki asked.

"What?"

"Why did you ..."

"Why did I kill Kawamura?"

"Yes."

"I killed him to avenge someone who died because of him."

In fact Baian had been paid one hundred fifty gold pieces by Hanemon to kill the samurai. But he believed the go-between when he had said, "The quicker that man is removed from the world, the better it will be for everyone."

It was Hanemon who had told him that Kawamura would be visiting the restaurant that day.

"I think it would be best if you were to tell me what it was you heard when Chubei told you to spy, but in order for you to do that, I will first have to make you trust me. I want you to think about it though—for your own sake. I'll come back the day after tomorrow to tend to your brother again."

Sudden Death

After two weeks of dedicated treatment, Sotaro's condition began to improve. Both Otoki and Sotaro's boss, Risuke, were of course delighted.

"I hope that you will not forget us in the future," he said, and arranged for a palanquin to carry Baian back to his house in Shinagawadai.

"When I get sick, I want you to make sure that Dr. Baian

is the one who treats me," Risuke told his wife.

Baian had been busy even before he took on Sotaro's case, but now he was rushed off his feet. Even after Sotaro took a turn for the better, he could not relax. He had to visit the other patients he had been neglecting.

It was a few days later that Baian heard that Otoki was dead —murdered.

When Baian had told her that she should stay at the Kagiya, she had decided to leave the Tachibanaya and accept a position in the shop as a live-in servant. A clerk from the Kagiya had gone to tell Chubei that Otoki would not be returning; Chubei had not seemed in the least put out. His apparent indifference had encouraged Otoki to visit the inn to get her things. She did not really care what happened to her clothes, but she did not want to lose her savings of fifty-seven gold pieces, which represented six years of hard work and degradation. She had hidden the cache somewhere on the grounds of the inn.

"I heard that you're going to live with your brother. I'm very happy for you," Chubei said with a smile when he met Otoki. "I know I can trust you, but remember, you must never tell anyone the things you've seen and heard while you were working here."

"Of course not."

Otoki was deliriously happy. She had always been terrified of Chubei and never thought it would be so easy to leave. She had been a bit scared of what would happen during her visit to the inn and had brought one of the Kagiya clerks with her.

"Phew, that's over then," the clerk said as they left. "I was scared he'd try and stop you."

"Yes, it's over now. I'm sorry to have dragged you all the way over here," Otoki apologized.

"Not at all."

They walked toward Akasaka in the spring sunshine, taking a shortcut through the fields of Takadanobaba.

A farmer found their bodies in a bamboo grove the following morning. The constables identified the clerk's body from an amulet around his neck. When they learned from the Kagiya that the two had gone to the Tachibanaya, the investigation moved there.

Chubei told the authorities that Otoki had come to pick up her things. He had seen them off himself and had no idea what had happened to them afterwards.

Otoki and the clerk had been stabbed, and, as her money was missing, the constables decided that it must have been the work of robbers. The case was closed for lack of evidence.

❖ ❖ ❖

Summer came. One afternoon soon after the end of the rainy season, Chubei visited Tokunosuke's pipe shop in Fukagawa to collect a silver pipe that he had ordered.

Tokunosuke had been an apprentice under the great craftsman Goto Heizaemon in Kyoto, and was now considered a master pipemaker in his own right. Chubei had placed the order two years earlier and was so excited about finally getting the pipe that he could barely wait to get home to try it.

That day he had attended a secret meeting in Akasaka with an official of the Kii clan, and although he had not expected the pipe to be ready, he had stopped by just in case. Delighted to hear that it was finished, he paid Tokunosuke ten gold pieces on account, and set off for home.

Everything is going well for me today, he thought.

Chubei left the craftsman's house and turned right into a narrow alley that led toward the main street, where he could hire a palanquin to take him home. The alleyway was only about four feet wide, and he was halfway down it when a man so large his shoulders seemed to brush the walls of the houses on either side appeared at the far end and began to walk toward him.

Chubei moved to one side to let the giant pass, his back pressed against the wall.

"Hot today, isn't it," the stranger said with a bow.

Chubei ignored him haughtily.

"Excuse me," the giant said as he turned sideways to try to pass him.

Those were the last words Chubei ever heard. As their chests brushed, Baian suddenly forced Chubei against the wall, his assassin's needle glinting in his right hand. Chubei's close-set eyes bulged in their sockets and his body stiffened against the wall.

Baian ran past Chubei down the alley, while Hikojiro, who had entered behind Chubei to cut off any possible escape, hurried back to the canal on the opposite side of the street, and jumped into a small boat he had ready there.

Two peddlers wearing large straw hats were walking along the road by the canal. One of them was carrying a load of mosquito nets on his back while the other cried out to advertise their wares.

Baian hurried out of the alley and jumped into the boat, casting a quick glance at the peddlers as he crossed the street. The small boat headed down the canal, while back in the alley Chubei's body slid slowly down the wall to the ground.

It was midday and very few people were on the streets. The two peddlers walked past the alley without so much as glancing down it.

"All the same," Hikojiro said as the boat moved into the

river, "do you really think it was Chubei who murdered Otoki?"

"Yes, he probably hired someone to do it. Otoki knew too many of his secrets for him to let her live."

"I agree with you there."

"In any case, the world will be a better place without him."

"It is a shame about Otoki, though," Hikojiro said. "She was all right—for a woman."

Hikojiro rowed through the heavy river traffic toward the Kitashinbori Wharf. Baian sat in the back, the hand he used to hold his assassin's needle trailing in the water. He held up a white fan to shade his eyes from the sun.

The white clouds of summer were piled high in the sky over Edo Bay.

FOUR KILLERS

The early summer sun shone on Atami, a spa town west of Edo. Baian relaxed on the grounds of a mountain shrine that overlooked the town, listening to the monotonous song of the cicadas in the surrounding trees. From the rock on which he sat he could see clouds of steam from the hot springs through the gateway of the shrine, and beyond, the sea, looking like a strip of blue paper pasted across the horizon.

Baian had come to Atami late that spring after murdering Kawamura, a corrupt samurai official of the Kii clan, at the request of the underworld boss Hanemon. He had been well paid for the job—fifty pieces of gold, enough for a family to live on for several years—so he was in no hurry to get back to work.

After Baian killed, he would go to a spa town, and rest for a while. The holiday not only helped him forget what he had done, it also strengthened him for his next job.

It's about time I got back to Edo and got down to work, he thought as he slowly got to his feet.

He still had a job waiting for him back in the city, and as he had already received an advance payment, he could not put it off any longer. A samurai was much more difficult to kill than a farmer or merchant. It took a lot of time and money to collect the necessary information, and then to make suitable preparations.

As Baian descended the steps from the shrine, he could feel energy flowing through his body. He had had his fill of good food, *sake*, and hot-spring baths. When he reached the bottom of the stairs, the afternoon sun glinted on his shaven head.

He walked through the town, past the stately official inn, where the great lords stayed when they visited the town, and on down the hill through the clouds of steam venting from the main spring. As he passed a small inn, a *ronin*—a samurai who knew no other master than his own sword— who had been sitting at an upstairs window, idly watching the passersby, gave a sudden start and drew back out of sight.

The seashore inn at which Baian was staying did not have a hot spring of its own, so morning and evening he would go into town to bathe at the main spring. Continuing back toward his inn, he did not notice the *ronin* slip into the street and begin to follow him.

The sun was setting. Baian went into his inn to pick up his towel, and on his way out told the landlord that he would be leaving the next day. It was dark when he walked past the *ronin*'s inn on his way to the baths. The brine of the sea mixed with the sulphur of the hot springs to create a heady aroma. As he walked, Baian passed a group of fishermen on their way home after a day at sea.

The *ronin*, back at his position by the window, watched Baian as he made his way up the hill. He was tall and muscular, but the white streaks in his carefully groomed hair showed him to be in his late forties. His forehead and cheeks were heavily furrowed, and his eyes burned with a fierce light.

A second, younger *ronin* came into the room on his way back from the bath. "What are you looking at, Inoue?" he asked.

"I was watching a man passing by on the road below."

"A man?"

"Yes, he's staying at an inn down near the shore. When I first saw him I thought I must have been mistaken. He's changed a lot since the last time we met, but I could never forget his face. No matter how hard I try, I can never forget."

"What did he do?"

"He murdered my wife."

"What?"

"It was ten years ago."

"I see why you can't forget."

Inoue said nothing.

"Do you want any help?" his younger, rather plump companion asked, but Inoue waved his hand to indicate that this would not be necessary.

"A hired killer is supposed to kill only for money, and I was quite happy to do just that until I saw him, but this is one job I'll enjoy doing free of charge. By the look of his clothes, he's still a doctor."

Baian Undercover

"It looks as though the rainy season has started," Baian

commented as he opened the window and looked out at the waterlogged garden. The pomegranate tree was in full bloom.

"You know, Hiko, I've never liked that flower," he muttered.

He and Hikojiro were sitting in the cottage in the rear garden of the Izutsu Restaurant, where he often stayed when he was in the city on a job. He had been there ten days now, but he had not set foot out the door since his arrival. He had come straight here after his return from Atami, pausing only briefly at his home on the way. Tonight he was joined by Hikojiro, whose house was nearby.

"How long are you going to stay here?"

"I'm not sure yet."

"Eh?"

"All I know is that someone followed me back to Edo from Atami and saw me enter my house."

"Are you sure you didn't just imagine it?"

"Yes, quite sure."

"Then who do you think it could be?"

"I don't know, I never got a chance to see him, but I've been in this business long enough to know when someone is on my tail."

"But don't you have any idea who it might have been?"

"No, it's ten years since I first became a hired killer, and though I must have killed about twenty people during that time, as far as I know no one could possibly identify me."

"Yes, it's the same for me."

"However, there is one man who knows about a woman I killed when I was a young man."

"Who is that?"

"Her husband."

"Oh…"

"Anyway, let's not talk about it now," Baian said, clapping his hands to call a waitress and order more *sake*. "When I left home to come here, two men tried to follow me, but I soon gave them the slip. There aren't many people who can follow me if I don't want them to."

"That's true."

"And ever since I arrived here, I haven't set foot out of the place."

"I didn't even know you were here myself."

"I'd like to ask you a favor."

"What is it? You know I'd be happy to help, and I don't expect anything in return. It will be a pleasure."

"I appreciate it, Hiko."

"Don't worry about it, it's my turn to help. Many's the time you've helped me with a job in the past, and I'm only too pleased for the opportunity to pay you back at last. What do you want me to do?"

"Kahei has asked me to kill a samurai called Ito, Lord Arima's personal secretary."

"A samurai, eh?...Sounds like a tough proposition."

"Yes, but he's willing to pay one hundred fifty pieces of gold to get the job done, and he assures me that the world will be a better place without him."

"All the same..."

"You couldn't check up on him, could you? See if you can find out anything that will give me an edge?"

"Leave it to me. I haven't got anything on at the moment, and I think it would be a good idea if you were to stay out of sight for a little longer."

"Thanks a lot, I knew I could rely on you," Baian said, placing a cloth-wrapped stack of twenty-five gold coins in front of Hikojiro.

"Well, if you insist." Hikojiro grinned and slipped the

money, cloth and all, into the front of his kimono just as the girl appeared with *sake*, noodles, and tuna *sashimi*.

After the waitress left, Baian put a sliver of raw fish into his mouth, then rubbed a bead of sweat from the side of his nose.

"You know, Hiko, I think my time's running out."

"Me too."

"I wonder if any hired killers live to see their old age?"

"I doubt it."

"So do I."

Lord Arima's Secretary

Lord Arima's residence was situated in an area of the city with many other lordly mansions, but it stood out in both size and splendor.

Baian's assigned victim, Ito, lived in the mansion. As Lord's Arima's personal secretary, he was in a position of great influence. Wherever Lord Arima went, Ito was constantly at his side. He dealt with people who wanted an audience, received gifts on behalf of his master, and arranged all necessary ceremonies. Although the position was hereditary, it took a very able person to fulfill its duties.

As he had such an important job, he always had a bodyguard with him when he left the mansion, and when he was on official business he was even permitted to use an enclosed palanquin, ordinarily reserved for the nobility.

A busy person like Ito would be very difficult to kill in secret. Baian could not do it when he went out on official business any more than he could enter the mansion unchallenged. If Ito were to come down with some kind of illness, Baian could take advantage of his reputation as an acupuncturist to get to him, but the secretary appeared to be in the best of health. He was fifty-three years old, plump, and without a gray hair on his head. He was a highly capable man and had the complete trust of his lord. His wife had borne him two sons and two daughters, and although his official income was not very high, his job offered enough extras to ensure that he lived a good life—a very good life.

Hikojiro took three days to find out this much. He had gone about the job in exactly the same way that Baian would have, visiting the restaurants and taverns around the mansion, pumping Lord Arima's retainers for information. Once they had had a few drinks, the lower retainers were more than happy to talk about their jobs to an attentive audience.

❖ ❖ ❖

"Thanks a lot, Hiko," Baian said.

"What do you mean? I've hardly started."

"You mean you'll stay on the job a bit longer?"

"Of course, this is only a beginning."

"Thanks, I really appreciate it. I know I should be doing this myself, but I think I should stay undercover a little longer."

"Do you really think that the man who's after you is the husband of the woman you killed?"

"I don't know, but I can't think of any other reason why anyone would be after me."

"You say he's a *ronin?*"

"Yes, and an expert swordsman."

"I see…"

"I've told you about my youth, haven't I? How I was adopted by a doctor from Kyoto after my mother abandoned me?"

"Yes."

"Well, after he died, I was all set to follow in his footsteps and become a good doctor, but I made one mistake."

"That woman?"

"Yes. It all started when I cured the wife of a poor *ronin* who lived behind the neighborhood temple."

"Was she good-looking?"

"You wouldn't believe how good."

"What do you mean?"

"Her body...I never knew a woman with a body like hers could exist."

"I don't believe it—you of all people," Hikojiro said with a snort of laughter.

"Her husband was a swordmaster and spent half of every month in Osaka practicing his art, so she was left on her own with too much time on her hands."

"Don't tell me."

"Yes, she seduced me. I couldn't resist. She threatened to tell her husband if I didn't become her lover."

"And I suppose the husband got to hear about it."

"Yes. When he asked his wife about it, she told him I had raped her."

"Women will say anything to get out of trouble."

"I was still young, it was more than ten years ago."

"What happened then?"

"The husband beat me with a staff—the wounds still trouble me in the winter." Baian put his hand to the small of his back and gave a bitter laugh. "I don't know why he didn't kill me—he would have been within his rights if he had. But even though he showed me mercy, I could not forgive his wife's lies. I killed her, using my needles to take life for the first time."

"Is that when you decided to become a hired killer?"

"Yes."

The two sat in silence.

It started to rain, and somewhere in the garden a tree frog began to cry out.

The Gambler

Baian had not been back to his house for ten days, and it was empty, except for Oseki's daily visits to do the cleaning.

The Lord of Sendai's mansion stood just to the east of Baian's house, surrounded by woods and fields. This was not his main Edo residence, but more of a country retreat, which he only rarely visited.

Although gambling was prohibited throughout the country, the city magistrates did not have jurisdiction over the possessions of the nobility. It was not unusual for servants in country mansions to use their masters' residences as gambling dens. The senior retainers all knew what was going on, but they turned a blind eye in exchange for a cut of the profits.

The Lord of Sendai was one of the most powerful lords in the country, and he owned numerous properties in Edo. Because it was very unlikely that he would ever find out what was going on in a minor holding—such as his mansion in Shinagawa—his footmen held gambling sessions there every three days.

A lone *ronin* had been staying there with the footmen for about six days now. He was a plump man in his thirties, who had come with an introduction from another lord's servant to join in the gambling.

It was not unusual for the servants to let their friends stay for as long as they liked, and so they were not at all surprised when on the first day he had said, "I like it here, would you mind if I stayed for a few more days?"

He was a good gambler, a heavy drinker, and very free

with his winnings, buying drinks for everyone and lending the others money when they ran out. His name was Sasaki, and he was the friend and traveling companion of Inoue, the *ronin* who had sworn to kill Baian.

Every afternoon Sasaki would leave the mansion by the back gate on business of his own, but when he returned in the evening he always brought a bottle of *sake*, which made him a popular guest among the servants.

Eleven days later, a middle-aged *ronin* came to the mansion's back gate.

"Is there a samurai by the name of Sasaki staying here?" Inoue asked.

"Yes, come in," the guard said, showing him to the servants' quarters without hesitation.

Sasaki and Inoue sat and talked in one corner of the room, sharing a bottle of *sake* while the servants gambled.

"He still hasn't gone back to his house," Sasaki reported, "I heard he was a good doctor, and his patients are eagerly waiting for his return."

"Damn. I've been searching too, but there's no sign of him anywhere. I wish now that we had killed him on the road back from Atami."

"But he knew we were on his tail."

"Exactly, that was the problem. If we'd tried to get him on the road, there was a good chance of his escaping."

"Yes, we never caught him off his guard."

Inoue sat in thought for a moment. "I don't think he's an ordinary doctor anymore. I'm sorry to have dragged you into this. After that job we did in Kyoto, I'd hoped we could spend six months looking around Edo and taking things easy."

"Don't worry about it. I'm more than happy to help you."

"You know..."

"What?"

"It occurred to me that perhaps Baian is a hired killer like us."

"You can't be serious."

"It's just a feeling I got when we were following him back from Atami."

Hikojiro's Luck

While Inoue and Sasaki were talking, Hikojiro was visiting Lord Arima's mansion only a short distance away. Here too the servants had opened a gambling den in one of the buildings, and Hikojiro had managed to get an invitation from a footman he had met in a nearby tavern. He had first made an appearance four nights earlier, and after that he had come every night, bringing a large bottle of *sake*. He was very free with his money and always had a funny story to tell, so in no time he had become a popular guest.

Hikojiro gambled for a while and then left the mansion at about nine o'clock. He had met the mansion's chief footman, Tomezo, only the previous evening. Hikojiro had plied him with drink and the two of them got on very well, but Hikojiro decided not to try to pump him for information straight away for fear of arousing Tomezo's suspicions. He thought he would wait until they became more friendly and Tomezo was completely at ease with him. When he went to the mansion that evening, however, he found that Tomezo was out on an errand and would not return until the following day.

It doesn't matter, I'm not in any hurry, Hikojiro said to himself as he stepped outside. He started to put up his umbrella, but looking up at the night sky, he realized that the rain had stopped.

Tucking the hem of his kimono into his sash, he set off
in clogs along the west side of the Satsuma clan's mansion
in the direction of the main road, a folded umbrella in his
left hand, a lantern in his right.

Baian's house was not far from the mansion, he remembered. He looked back and noticed a shadowy figure walking up the hill behind him. It was a tall, well-built *ronin*.

Hikojiro froze to the spot. He could not know that this
was Inoue—who had just come out of the Lord of Sendai's
mansion—any more than Inoue could have guessed that
Hikojiro was Baian's only friend. They stood for a moment
on the unlit street, glaring at each other, every nerve
tensed. The only possible explanation for their behavior
was that, because they were hired killers, their senses were
sharper than those of ordinary people.

Suddenly Inoue moved forward, passing on Hikojiro's
right. The look in his eye as they passed was enough to
make Hikojiro tighten his grip on his umbrella. He did not
move until Inoue's figure disappeared into the night, then
he began to tremble from head to foot.

I wonder if that was the swordsman who's after Baian, he
thought suddenly. He might have been spying on Baian's
house.

The following day Hikojiro went to the Izutsu Restaurant
to see Baian and told him about the previous night's
events. After he had described the *ronin*'s features and
clothes, Baian nodded.

"I was right then." He did not seem to be very surprised.
"So this time the roles are reversed, and I'm the one that is
to be killed."

"He did not look like an ordinary *ronin*. I think he's
killed many people in his time."

"That wouldn't surprise me."

"I might be wrong, but I think he may be a hired killer like us."

"There's always that chance."

"What are you going to do?"

"For the time being, I think I'll stay right here."

It had not rained since the previous night, and the sun shone weakly through ragged clouds. The two men sat drinking *sake* in silence.

"Are you going to go to Lord Arima's mansion again tonight, Hiko?"

"I was planning to. Tomezo, the head footman I told you about, should be back tonight. If I get him drunk and lend him some money for gambling, I'm sure he won't mind telling me the gossip about Ito."

Three days later, Hikojiro returned to the Izutsu. Baian was cleaning his acupuncture needles with alcohol and laying them out to dry.

"You know, I have had a very stiff shoulder and back lately," Hikojiro said.

"Why didn't you mention it earlier! Come here, I'll have a look."

Baian made Hikojiro lie down. After running his hands down his back, he inserted several needles along his spine.

"How's that?" he asked. "It doesn't hurt, does it?"

"No, it doesn't. You know, it's the first time I've ever had acupuncture."

"You don't eat properly. You live on your own and only eat when you feel like it. Your stomach can't take such abuse indefinitely, you know."

"What do you mean?"

"Yes. Just because you like tofu doesn't mean that you

should eat it morning, noon, and night. You should also eat plenty of vegetables to balance your diet."

"Is that so?"

"There, that feels better, doesn't it?"

"Yes, it does, thanks."

"Let's get drunk tonight."

"Yes, let's do that. By the way, I managed to find out a bit more about Ito."

"Good."

It had started to rain again.

Baian got up and went to the kitchen to order some food and *sake*. As he came back into the room, he said, "It's very chilly out today. I hate the rainy season."

"Yes, it depresses the hell out of me, too."

"I've got a treat for you, Hiko. I've ordered all the things you're not eating enough of."

A short while later, a waitress entered carrying an earthenware dish on top of a small charcoal brazier. In the dish was a stew of thick slices of white radish and fried tofu.

"The soup's made with chicken stock," Baian said. "Try it and tell me what you think."

"Mmm…not bad."

"It makes a nice change, doesn't it?"

"Yes. You know, this is really good," Hikojiro said, ladling a large helping into a bowl.

"Now, what did you manage to find out?"

"Well, this Ito you've been contracted to kill is a very powerful man in the mansion. He's Lord Arima's favorite, and even the chamberlain doesn't dare cross him. There's no mistake about it, I got it from the chief footman himself. And Ito doesn't hesitate to take advantage of his position to throw his weight around."

It seemed that Ito was blackmailing the merchants who

dealt with Lord Arima. They had to pay him huge bribes in order to keep doing business with the clan. In the normal run of things, the chamberlain and other high officials, who were usually picked from the lord's family, would have put an end to such outrageous behavior. Recently, however, corruption had spread like a cancer throughout the Arima household.

Ito had inherited his position as secretary while the present lord's father was still alive, and had gone to great lengths to curry favor with the young lord to be. When the old lord died, Ito suddenly became one of the most influential people in the Arima clan, but he did not seek promotion. He was happy to keep his present post while amassing a fortune for himself.

Many other retainers dealt with the merchants, but Ito was the only one who had a personal connection with the lord, and the merchants were willing to pay for access. He also helped the lord to slip out of the mansion in disguise occasionally, enabling him to sample delights that were generally were not available to someone of his rank. This only put Ito higher in his master's esteem. Although the chamberlain and the elders knew what was going on, they could do nothing to put a stop to it because Ito was shrewd enough to share some of his gains with the other officials.

"Well, that's about it so far," Hikojiro said.

"Thank you very much. I'm beginning to see what it's all about now."

"By the way, I hear Ito is quite a regular at the Suigetsuro Restaurant in Kobikicho."

"Oh really ... that's very interesting."

"Have you worked out how you are going to do it?"

"More or less."

"That's good to hear."

"I don't like asking, but could you help me a little more?"

"Of course. I've come this far, and to tell the truth, I'm rather enjoying myself."

"I tell you what, after we finish this job and I get the remaining seventy-five pieces of gold from Kahei, why don't the two of us go on a pilgrimage to the Grand Shrine at Ise?"

"Do you really mean it?"

"Why not? It will make a change. We can go away and forget everything for a while."

"I'd love to go, but what about you? Do you really want to waste all your earnings like that?"

"Waste? Easy come, easy go! Anyway, as far as society is concerned our whole profession is a waste."

"Too true," Hikojiro said with a laugh, raising his *sake* cup. "All the same, you should be careful of this Inoue character."

"Yes, speaking of Inoue…"

"I'll handle the Ito job if you like," Hikojiro offered.

"No, that's all right, I'll deal with him myself, but would you mind if I asked another favor of you?"

"Ask away."

The Stratagem

While Baian was away, Oseki came in every day to look after his house. She was married to one of the local farmers, but because her daughter-in-law did the housework at home, she had plenty of time to herself. Baian paid her well for what she did, and she was happy to look after him, doing the washing and making sure the house was kept clean.

She would arrive in the morning and stay until evening, busying herself with needlework and other chores. She had no idea when Baian would put in an appearance, but she always kept fresh water and firewood close to hand to be able to prepare a bath for him at a moment's notice.

The people in the neighborhood were all eagerly awaiting his return, the clogmaker Kinzo among them. Baian had cured him of a fever earlier that year, but the rainy season had put him back in bed.

"Damn that Baian," he cursed. "It will serve him right if I'm dead by the time he gets back."

He made such a fuss that his wife was at her wit's end.

❖ ❖ ❖

One day there was a break in the clouds and the sun broke through to produce one of those glorious hot, sunny days that occur so rarely during the rainy season. In the farms to the south, as well as in the merchants' houses squeezed between the samurai mansions, the women were all hard at work, happy for the chance to get some laundry done.

Oseki had gone home shortly after noon and did not return until almost two o'clock. When she reached the gate of the shrine next to Baian's house, a short, plump *ronin* walking in the opposite direction passed her. She had noticed him several times hanging around the shrine in the past few days, but she did not give him any thought. He was well-dressed, and there was nothing about his behavior to put her on guard.

Their eyes met, but he was quite relaxed, and she guessed that he was probably staying at one of the mansions in the neighborhood.

"Lovely weather we're having," she remarked, bowing her graying head. The *ronin* smiled in reply and continued on down the road.

Oseki hurried through the trees to the house to find a man waiting outside for her.

"Are you Oseki?" he asked. It was Hikojiro.

"Yes, I am."

"I came with a message from Dr. Baian," he announced in a loud voice.

"What, really? Where is the doctor now?"

"He had some business in Fukagawa, but he asked me to tell you that he would be returning the day after tomorrow, at six o'clock in the evening, and he wants you to have the bath ready for him when he gets back."

"Yes, yes, tell him not to worry."

"He also asked me to tell you to buy a bottle of *sake* for that night."

"Six o'clock the day after tomorrow," Oseki repeated.

"That's right, he'll be coming home around that time."

"Can you tell him that half the neighborhood is waiting for him to come back?"

"Certainly. I'll be going now."

Hikojiro hurried off.

About two hours later Oseki was just thinking of returning home when someone came to the door.

"Is there anyone home?"

Oseki hurried out to find the plump *ronin* she had seen that afternoon standing at the front door.

"Oh, hello," Oseki said.

"I was told that I would be able to find a good doctor here."

"Yes, that's correct."

"I'm staying at Lord Arima's mansion, but recently I've been having some trouble with my stomach."

"I'm afraid that the doctor isn't here at the moment, but I had a message from him this afternoon saying that he would be returning the day after tomorrow."

"The day after tomorrow, you say?"

"Yes, he won't be back until about six o'clock, but you needn't worry, he'll see you in the evening if you ask him to."

"I'll do that, thank you."

The *ronin* walked away.

The *ronin* was of course Sasaki. From his hiding place in the shrine, he had watched Hikojiro arrive and leave. Wondering what the man had come for, Sasaki had decided to approach Oseki in person to see what she could tell him. That evening, in the servant's quarters at Lord Arima's mansion, he told Inoue everything he had managed to learn.

Inoue sat in silent thought.

"Do you suppose he thinks we've given up, and that it's safe for him to return home now?"

"I don't know."

"What will you do?"

"I'd have thought that was obvious. I'm not going to let him get away again. That is, if the man you saw was telling the truth and Baian really is going home."

"You can count on me," Sasaki said.

"If we're not careful, he might get away again. I should have killed him ten years ago when I found out what he'd done. But I didn't, I forgave him, and he repaid me by killing her. I hate him. I'll never forgive him for that."

"You must have loved your wife very much."

Inoue did not reply.

❖ ❖ ❖

In the cottage in the garden of the Izutsu, Baian and Hikojiro shared a drink as they talked quietly. Baian produced a small clothbound parcel.

"I've put everything in here for you, Hiko," he said as he passed it over.

"It's a long time since I used one of these," Hikojiro said, picking up the parcel.

Late that night Hikojiro left the restaurant and hired a boat to take him downriver. After Hikojiro had gone, Baian called the waitress.

"Don't wake me tomorrow, please," he said. After she left, he took out three four-inch assassin's needles and started to sharpen them.

The rain had started again, but Baian did not spare a glance in the direction of the door. He was totally absorbed by his task, his eyes narrow slits below his bulging forehead.

Omon

The next day Baian did not wake until almost noon.

As soon as she realized he was awake, Omon, one of the waitresses, hurried over from the main building bringing hot water for him to wash with. Until that day Baian had paid no particular attention to her, but suddenly he called out to her and held her hand.

"It's all right, isn't it?" he asked, staring hard into her eyes. She did not move.

Omon was thirty-five years old. She had a nine-year-old son who lived with her father while she worked at the Izutsu. Her husband was dead, and though she was a hard worker, she spoke little and kept very much to herself.

"But...but..." she said, trying to pull away, but looking down at Baian's broad chest and strong shoulders, she felt her resolution weaken.

Baian did not say a word. He sat staring at her, his eyes burning with emotion. Omon felt her power to resist flowing away.

Baian pulled her down toward him, encircling her with one strong arm while his other hand slipped inside her kimono to fondle her breasts. They were fuller than he had expected.

"No, please…"

"It's all right."

"But…"

"Don't worry."

The strength seemed to run out of Omon's limbs and she could not resist any longer.

When Baian finally let her go, she ran out of the room, hiding her face behind the sleeve of her kimono. She straightened her clothing and hurried back to the main building without saying a word.

A different waitress brought his lunch, but Baian did not ask her what had happened to Omon.

The rain continued throughout the day, and Baian stayed in his room, lying on the quilts, doing nothing.

That night it was Omon who brought him his *sake*.

Baian stayed in bed and did not turn to face her.

"Are you angry about this morning?" he asked.

"I was just a bit surprised," Omon replied. Her voice was richer than before, and she sounded a different person altogether.

"I suddenly…I suddenly…" Baian murmured.

"What is it?"

"When I woke up this morning, I suddenly felt I was going to die."

"What are you talking about? You're still in your thirties."

Baian was astounded that Omon should suddenly become so talkative.

"That's why…why…" It was Baian who was too flustered

to speak. "That's why I wanted you. I felt that this was the end, and I was so lonely."

"What are you talking about?" Omon sat down beside him, pressing her body against his. "Would you like some *sake*?"

Baian sat up and kissed the back of her neck. She smelled of makeup, which he had never known her to wear until then.

Later that night Omon crept into Baian's room. Her passion amazed him, and he realized how much she had been holding back since her husband's death.

❖ ❖ ❖

While Baian was with Omon at the restaurant, Hikojiro sneaked into his house. Oseki had locked up when she left, but it was a simple task for him to open one of the kitchen shutters with a narrow-bladed knife.

Baian certainly lives in style, he thought.

Although the house was not large, with the kitchen and the two tatami-mat rooms in the back separated from an earthen-floored entrance hall by a small wooden-floored room, Hikojiro could tell that the whole building had been constructed with exquisite taste and the best materials.

He moved aside one of the ceiling boards in the wooden-floored room, lit a candle, and opened the bag he had brought with him. Inside was the package that Baian had given him at the restaurant the previous evening, a short sword, five riceballs wrapped in bamboo leaves, and a bamboo water canteen. He stood on a low stool and carefully stowed everything in the loft, then he pulled out Baian's bed and went to sleep.

The next morning, after clearing away the bedding, he fetched an empty basin from the kitchen and then climbed into the loft using a rope he had tied around two of the rafters in the attic the previous night. He pulled the rope up behind him, leaving no trace of his presence.

Once he was settled, he ate two of the riceballs and drank a little of the water. At around noon, he heard Oseki arrive and begin to tidy the house. The rain made a muted noise as it struck the thatched roof.

Hikojiro dozed off and did not awaken until he heard Oseki moving around below him.

I expect Baian will be home any minute now, he thought with a grin. He ate three more riceballs and had another drink of water. He then used the wooden basin to relieve himself, being careful not to make any noise that might be heard below. Finally, he opened the package Baian had given him and started to sort through its contents.

A little while later, he heard Baian return by palanquin.

"Oh doctor, where have you been all this time?" Oseki asked.

"Is the bath ready?"

"Yes, it should be ready any minute now."

"I'm sorry I've been away so long. Here take this. It's a small gift to thank you for looking after the place for me."

"Oh, thank you, doctor."

Oseki was in the house until Baian went in for his bath. She cooked a meal and warmed a flask of *sake* for him when he got out.

"Well, I'll see you tomorrow," she called out as she left the house.

Baian waited until he was sure she had gone, then walked to the wooden-floored room and called out softly.

"Are you there, Hiko?"

"Yes, don't worry."

"I'm sorry to put you through this."

"Don't worry. After all, it was only for one day."

"Why don't you come down for a bit?"

"No, we must stay on our guard, there's no telling when they might attack."

"That's true, but I hope you won't mind if I have a hot meal down here."

"Not at all."

"I'll be sleeping on the wooden floor tonight."

"Right you are, I can see you very well there."

"Thanks, Hiko."

"Not at all, I'm rather enjoying myself."

"If anything happens to me, I want you to try to get away, all right?"

"Whatever you say."

Uninvited Callers

As the night deepened, the rain came down harder.

Baian dragged his bedding to the wooden-floored room, directly under Hikojiro's hiding place, and lay down fully-clothed. He had lit a lantern in the larger of the two matted rooms where he usually slept, but he used no light in the room he was in nor in the earthen-floored hallway by the front door. The wooden-floored room was separated from the hall by translucent paper doors. A set of identical doors led to the lighted room; Baian had left these open.

Time passed, but nothing happened.

"Hiko," Baian said, looking up at the ceiling.

"Shh! We mustn't talk anymore. They're going to come, I'm sure of it."

"You think so?"

"Yes, I can feel it in my bones."

"Me too."

"This is it then."

"I am very seldom wrong about such things."

"Me either."

"I'm as ready as I'll ever be."

"We mustn't talk anymore."

Eventually even the sound of the rain stopped.

Suddenly, a tap sounded from the ceiling above Baian's bed. It was a warning from Hikojiro.

Two of the ceiling boards slid away silently . The attic was pitch black, but Baian could see the whites of Hikojiro's eyes shining in the dark.

Baian had also sensed their coming. The sound of two pairs of sandaled feet came through the night. The two men separated: One went around the back, while the other continued to the front. Baian's body tensed as he strained to listen.

If he had been asleep he would not have heard a thing. Just the sound of sandals on the rain-drenched earth, and it was only years of practice allowed Baian's and Hikojiro's sharpened senses to notice it.

The footsteps stopped.

There was a moment of breathless silence, and then the night was rent by the sound of the front and back doors being smashed open simultaneously. The intruders must have thrown their full weight against the doors.

Sasaki, who had come in through the front, kicked open the paper doors leading to the wooden-floored room, but he was not expecting to find Baian waiting for him there.

Even as the *ronin* cried out, Baian kicked aside the bedding and flung himself at him, grasping him with tremendous strength.

Sasaki's cry of dismay came just as the second *ronin*, who had smashed his way in through the back door, burst through the screens leading to the illuminated room. He was silhouetted against the light, and Hikojiro could see that it was Inoue.

The *ronin* cursed. His prey was not where he had expected him to be, and now he stood exposed in the light. He hesitated for a few seconds, his sword raised, searching for a target to strike. As he did so, he heard the noise of Baian and Sasaki crashing to the floor. He turned in that direction, but suddenly there was a sharp hiss from the ceiling. Flashes of light glinted in the dark, and something struck him in the eye and throat.

Hikojiro was using a blowpipe to shoot darts at him from his hiding place in the attic.

Inoue cried out in pain. He tried to find cover in the shadows, but the darts came unrelentingly, until finally two hit him in the back of the neck. Inoue dropped his sword and collapsed to the floor. As he fell, there was a groan from the other room as Baian finished off Sasaki.

❖ ❖ ❖

Late next morning Oseki came to the house to find everything in its place.

"You can go home after you've finished the cleaning," Baian said from his bed in the larger matted room.

"Thank you. By the way, doctor, did a plump *ronin* come to see you last night?"

"What?" Baian said with a start. "No, nobody came."

"That's strange, he said that he had a bad stomach and would be coming to see you."

"Oh really."

"He said that he was staying in the servants' quarters at Lord Arima's mansion."

"Lord Arima's mansion?"

"I wonder what happened to him? I suppose his stomach

must have stopped bothering him."

"Yes, that's probably it," Baian said with a laugh.

Ito's Last Meal

Lord Arima's secretary died one evening soon after the end of the rainy season.

A merchant had invited him to dinner at his favorite restaurant, the Suigetsuro in Kobikicho. The host sent a palanquin to pick him up, and Ito arrived a little after four in the afternoon.

The two men discussed business for about an hour, but once that was finished they started to drink. They had geisha to entertain them, and Ito was in high spirits when he stood up to go to the toilet.

One of the geisha began to walk him down the corridor, but he waved her away. He knew the building well.

Ito never returned to the party.

"What can have happened to him?" the merchant said after some time had passed. "One of you go and see."

One of the girls hurried to the toilet at the end of the corridor.

It was a very pretty toilet. An anteroom with a stone floor led to a delicate door, half wood and half translucent paper. The toilet was on the other side of the door, and the air in the small cubicle was always filled with the smell of incense.

There was no sign of anyone in the anteroom, but when the girl slid the door open, she screamed and fainted.

Ito was lying face up on the floor. When they examined the body, they found a small wound—which could have been made by a needle—just over his heart.

❖ ❖ ❖

Two weeks later, Baian and Hikojiro were walking down

the Tokaido, the main highway linking Edo and Kyoto. They both wore traveling clothes and had walked almost two hundred miles from Edo to the village of Chiriu. The sky was blue, and the clouds were piled high in the distance.

They were going to walk as far as Atsuta, where they would catch a ferry to Kuwana, then continue to the Grand Shrine at Ise. After visiting the shrine they planned to go on through Nara, Osaka, and Kyoto, sightseeing as they went.

"Baian," Hikojiro said.

"What?"

"Why on earth are we making a pilgrimage to Ise?"

"I don't know."

"Neither do I."

"Our hands are so stained with other people's blood that I don't think we'll ever be able to wash them clean, even in the waters of Ise."

"No mistake."

"So I ended up killing both Inoue and his wife."

"What are you talking about? I got him with my blowpipe."

"Yes, I suppose that's true."

"Everything went well after all. I was amazed when I heard you'd finished the Ito job so quickly. How on earth did you manage it?"

"It wasn't that hard. And the money I got from Kahei for the job ought to last us at least six months."

"This will be my first time in Kyoto."

"So you said."

Baian's face clouded over suddenly, and he said, "Hiko, I feel like I'm going to die before long."

"Me too. All hired killers probably feel that way."

They walked on in silence for a while before Baian spoke again.

"The noodles in the village we're coming to are really rather special," he said with a grin.

AUTUMN JOURNEY

The autumn flowers by the roadside were in full bloom. Night was beginning to fall. Baian stopped and turned to Hikojiro. "The summer's coming to an end at last," he said sadly.

"Yes, but what a summer it's been."

"How long has it been since we left Edo?"

"About forty days, isn't it?"

"You're right," Baian replied, counting on his fingers.

"It's difficult to keep track, isn't it? The way we've been living."

"Yes, but I don't think I've ever had a better time."

"Me either."

To see them standing there, looking at the autumn flowers, no one could have ever guessed that they were hired killers. Baian wore an expensive kimono, with a decorated short sword tucked into the sash, and carried a bamboo staff. His head was neatly shaved and covered with a conical lacquered hat that made him look every inch the doctor that he was. Although Hikojiro was just as well dressed, everyone who saw them automatically assumed that he was Baian's servant.

They had been on the road since early summer, enjoying the local specialties and *sake* wherever they stopped. They had taken a boat across Ise Bay, then traveled to the Grand Shrine of the Sun Goddess. After their pilgrimage, they visited the famous red-light district in Furuichi, where they stayed for ten days.

Hikojiro particularly had enjoyed himself. "Our visit to the shrine was definitely not a waste of time," he said with a lewd grin. "The goddess certainly answered my prayers!"

After their stay in Furuichi, they resumed their journey to Kyoto on the Tokaido road, traveling as far as Kameyama, where they turned off into Iga and Yamato provinces.

Yamato was famous not only for its many shrines and temples but also for its scenery, which was unlike any other in Japan. It lay in a shallow basin surrounded by beautiful mountains. This was Hikojiro's first visit, and he found everything new and wonderful. Baian, on the other hand, had been brought up in Kyoto and had traveled the area extensively with his teacher, Etsudo. He was able to point out all the places of interest.

They were enjoying their trip, and though they both had a well-developed sixth sense when it came to danger, neither realized that, even as they spoke, fate was hurrying along the road behind them.

They stopped to see the giant Buddha at the Todaiji Temple and the Kasuga Shrine in Nara, then continued toward the Utahime Pass, preferring the old road from Nara to Kyoto to the more crowded modern one.

"I see what you mean, Baian," Hikojiro said, looking around him. "This road is just perfect for people like us who don't want to be noticed."

There were very few other travelers on the old highway, and the vegetation was encroaching on its edges, waiting for the time when it would reclaim the road.

"It's getting late. Where are we going to stay tonight?" Hikojiro asked.

"We could turn off onto the main road and stay at Kizu if you like, but I know a place further along the road. You won't be able to enjoy any women or *sake*, but you'll be able to get a good night's sleep for a change."

"Do you mean a temple?"

"Exactly."

"Is it far?"

"No, it's in a village a little further down the road. The temple is called Jonenji and although the abbot died several years ago, I once treated him. I've stayed there many times over the years, but not since I started my present career."

The sun began to set, yet the dusk retained the warmth of summer.

"Anyway, we'd better hurry if we want to arrive before dark," Baian said.

They were about to move on, when a middle-aged samurai overtook them. Hikojiro glanced at him as he passed, and a look of shock came into his eyes. He stopped where he was and stared after the man.

"Come on," Baian said, turning back. "What is it, Hiko?"

Hikojiro did not reply.

"What is it?" Realizing that something was wrong, he hurried to his friend's side. The samurai continued down the road without so much as a glance back at them.

"Hikojiro?"

"That bastard..." The voice that issued from Hikojiro's

throat was so distorted by emotion that it sounded like someone else.

"That bastard? You mean that samurai?"

Hikojiro nodded.

"He's got to die."

Hikojiro's Story

This was not the right time for Baian to find out what the problem was, but he knew Hikojiro well enough to realize that it was something serious. The samurai hurried into the distance, and without any further discussion the two friends set off in pursuit.

They walked in silence.

"He probably doesn't remember me," Hikojiro said, increasing his pace until they were not far behind the man.

The evening grew darker, but after walking almost another league, their prey showed no sign of stopping.

"Where the hell is that bastard going to stay?"

"It's getting late so I expect he's planning to stay at Tanabe."

"Is it far?"

"Only another league or so."

They walked on in silence.

"What did he do to you?" Baian asked quietly.

"He killed my wife and daughter."

"What?" Baian tensed. He still did not know the details, but he understood. Hikojiro was right—the samurai had to die.

Night had fallen by the time they reached Tanabe. Although it was only a small village, being situated on the old highway between Nara and Kyoto, it boasted two inns and a *sake* manufacturer.

The samurai entered one of the inns.

"What do you want to do?" Baian asked, wondering if they should stay at the other inn.

Hikojiro shook his head. "It's all right. Even if he sees me, I doubt that he'd recognize me now."

The inn was a small, one-storied building with only five rooms. The samurai stayed in a room at the rear of the building, and Baian and Hikojiro were given the room two doors down from his. The samurai went to the bath first, and they waited until he had finished before they entered.

Once they had returned to their room, they relaxed and sat down for their evening meal. They knew that the samurai would not be going anywhere that night, and they had until the following day to decide what their next move was going to be.

That night Hikojiro started to tell Baian his story.

He had been born the son of a poor farmer in Matsudo, not far from Edo. His father had died when he was six years old, and his mother soon found another man to come and live with her.

"I never wanted to have you from the beginning," she told Hikojiro one day, as though it were his fault that he had been born.

He put up with this treatment until he was ten years old, then ran away from home. By that time his mother had given birth to two more children by her second husband, and Hikojiro's position in the household had gotten worse by the day.

"It's the first time you've ever told me about your past," Baian said with a sympathetic smile. "It's very similar to my own in a way, don't you think?"

Hikojiro did not tell him how he spent the remaining years of his childhood and adolescence, but when he turned twenty-one, he finally found peace.

A merchant called Sakubei found him living rough in the streets and arranged for him to be taken in by a temple in Magome.

"I owe him everything," Hikojiro said ruefully.

Hikojiro lived in a small house on the temple grounds and worked hard to repay his benefactors, cleaning the buildings and tending the temple's fields. He so impressed the priests that the following year, when he turned twenty-two, they arranged for him to marry the daughter of one of the local farmers, an eighteen-year-old girl called Ohiro. The following year, the couple had a daughter.

"When I look back over that period of two or three years, I find it hard to believe it really happened to me. It was the first time I ever knew what it meant to be really happy."

His happiness, however, was not to last; tragedy set Hikojiro on the road to becoming a hired killer.

One day he had been working in the fields since morning. The country around Magome was rugged, and the field where he worked was in a deep valley, surrounded by steep cliffs and tall trees. Around noon his wife appeared with some rice balls and pickles for lunch.

When they had first married, she was so thin that Hikojiro worried that something was wrong with her, but after she had her first child, her bust and hips filled out, and it was hard to believe that she was only nineteen years old.

"Where's the baby?"

"She was sleeping so soundly I left her in the house."

The two sat together in the shade of the trees and started to eat. Ohiro undid the collar of her kimono to let the air in, and he could see the top of her breasts. Her neck and arms were tanned, but, in comparison, her breasts seemed almost translucent in their paleness. Still holding a rice ball in one hand, Hikojiro bent over and kissed her neck.

"Stop it, you're tickling me."

"Ohiro."

"Yes?"

"I hope we have a boy next time."

"We can have as many as you want. Stop it! Not here."

"Why not?"

"But…"

"Nobody's looking."

Unfortunately he was mistaken.

Two *ronin* suddenly jumped down the cliff behind them. They smelled of sweat, their clothes were filthy, and their hair was dirty and unkempt.

"Hand the woman over to us for a while," one of them demanded with an ominous laugh.

"Run! quickly!" Hikojiro cried, his face pale as he rose to his feet.

"Stay out of this if you want to live," the other *ronin* said as he approached him threateningly, his eyes flashing like a mad dog's.

"Help!" Ohiro tried to run, but the first *ronin* hit her in the stomach and knocked her to the ground.

"What do you think you're doing?!" Hikojiro cried, and rushed at the man, but the *ronin* drew his sword and hit him with the flat of the blade. That was the last thing he knew. When he came to, Ohiro was lying half naked under one of the *ronin* as he thrust into her repeatedly, delighting in the pain he was inflicting.

"Ah! You bastard!" Hikojiro attempted to get up, but his arms and legs were numb, and his head felt as though it would burst. When he tried to move, the other man, who had been waiting his turn, beat him into unconsciousness again.

"I was a different person in those days, Baian. There was

101

nothing I could do," Hikojiro explained. "Nothing was ever the same after that. Six days later... six days later, she hung herself."

"She killed herself?"

"Yes, and that's not all. Before she died, she—she killed our daughter."

Baian turned pale.

"She went crazy. They had done more than just rape her."

When he finished speaking there were no tears in his eyes—only hatred.

"And that person who is staying in the back room, he was one of the two *ronin*?"

"Yes."

"Which one?"

"The one with the eyes of a mad dog."

"I wonder if he still has the same friend."

"We should try and find out. I'd like to pay them both back for what they did, if it's humanly possible."

"In that case we shouldn't do anything tonight. Let's follow him and see if he leads us to his accomplice."

"I agree."

"You helped me out last time, so now it's my turn to repay you."

"Thank you. We're a long way from Edo, and I wouldn't know how to get around without you."

Last time, Hikojiro had helped Baian kill a *ronin* who wanted revenge for the death of his wife, and now Baian was going to help Hikojiro get revenge for the very same thing.

"It's a strange world, isn't it? Everything seems to come down to women in the end," Baian said, sipping cold *sake*. "I can't tell you how sorry I am to hear about your wife and daughter," he added. His voice trembled, and his eyes flashed with cold rage.

The Chase

The following morning Hikojiro and Baian ate an early breakfast and packed their belongings so that they could leave at a moment's notice. They sat in their room with the doors closed, waiting for the samurai to walk by in the corridor as he went out. The sound of his footsteps indicated that he was oblivious to the fact that he was being followed.

"Let's go," Hikojiro said, getting up.

"There's no hurry," Baian replied. He clapped his hands to summon the maid. "Here's something for you," he said, giving her a generous tip even though he had already tipped her the previous evening. He asked her to bring the inn's register and waited until she left the room to open it.

There had been only two other guests in the inn the previous night, a merchant and the samurai. They had no trouble in discovering the name of their quarry. He had signed his name as Mineyama Matajuro, a retainer to Lord Matsudaira of Wakayama, and he wrote in a powerful, flowing script.

"Are you quite sure this is the man you're after?" Baian asked quietly as he closed the register.

"Do you think I could make a mistake about a thing like this?"

"Of course not, it's just…"

"Baian, we'd better get going or we might lose the bastard."

"Don't worry, I know the area. Just leave it to me."

They left the inn, and soon after saw Mineyama on the road ahead of them.

"Hiko, I know it was twenty years ago," Baian said as they

walked, "but I still cannot relate the man we're following with the beast who raped your wife."

"Why not?"

The Lord of Wakayama was one of the most powerful lords in the country, and Mineyama looked every inch one of his retainers. Baian had never seen the man who had raped Ohiro, but Hikojiro had said that he was like a wild animal, and yet the man they were following was neatly dressed, well-mannered, and obviously well educated. He wondered if a person could change that much, even in twenty years.

Hikojiro is quite certain, so there can be no mistake, Baian told himself. But he had to repeat it several times before he could convince himself.

Mineyama did not look back once.

The samurai's steps seemed a little heavier than on the previous day, but Hikojiro did not seem to notice. He simply kept his gaze fixed on his quarry, his eyes burning with rage.

The road they were on was very narrow, and had little traffic, so they kept quite a distance between themselves and the samurai. Sometimes they would even allow him to drop out of sight for a while, but they knew that there was nowhere he could go, and he soon came into view again.

Baian tried to make small talk, but Hikojiro was so intent on the pursuit that he did not notice. Baian was surprised: he had known Hikojiro for many years, and they had been through a lot together, but in all that time he had never before known him to lose control like this. That was when he realized the extent of the hatred that Hikojiro had been nursing for so long.

They came to the famous Hachiman Shrine about six miles north of Tanabe. The shrine stood on a mountain peak where the Katsura, Uji, and Kizu rivers joined to form the Yodo River.

In the middle of the ninth century, a holy man named Gyokyo had had a dream in which the war god Hachiman told him to build a shrine on the site. The members of the imperial court all worshiped there, and it soon became the second most holy site in the country after the Grand Shrine at Ise. A thriving town had sprung up outside the shrine gates, with many restaurants and inns to cater for the numerous pilgrims who came to pray.

Mineyama arrived a little before noon. After resting in one of the teahouses for about an hour, he left his luggage there, crossed the bridge over the river, and began the climb to the shrine. He obviously meant to pray there before continuing his journey.

Watching from one of the other teahouses nearby, Baian again could not reconcile the image of the bestial *ronin* with this well-behaved gentleman.

"Hiko."

"Yes?"

"Are you sure you are not letting your emotions get the better of you?"

"You may be right, but I'm afraid there's nothing I can do about it."

"Do you think that the samurai realizes we're following him?"

"I don't know."

"He hasn't looked back once, and he didn't see us at the inn last night."

"That's true. I hadn't really thought about it."

"Stay here, will you?"

"What are you going to do?"

"Leave it to me. I have an idea."

Their eyes locked for a moment, then Hikojiro nodded. "All right, I'll be waiting for you here."

Baian's Hunch

Baian followed Mineyama up the mountain to the shrine. He had put on weight during the trip, and he panted as he hurried after the much fitter samurai.

Finally arriving at the ancient shrine, Mineyama bowed his head in prayer. As soon as he had finished, he turned and immediately started to make his way back down the mountain.

Baian also offered a quick prayer before continuing pursuit. The number of pilgrims on the stairs had increased, and the sun was so hot that Baian was drenched with sweat before he had gotten halfway down. He had hoped to talk to Mineyama without Hikojiro seeing him, but he found himself back at the foot of the mountain before the chance presented itself.

Hikojiro was watching from the teahouse when Baian arrived, panting from the exertion.

"How was it?"

"I don't know yet."

"What do you mean, you don't know? There's nothing to know apart from the fact that he killed my wife and daughter."

"Yes, I realize that."

"If you don't want to help me, you can just get lost, all right?" Hikojiro said with a flash of anger. He obviously felt that Baian's heart was not really in the job.

Baian smiled sadly, and Hikojiro immediately regretted what he had said. "I'm sorry, I didn't mean it."

"That's all right, don't worry about it."

Mineyama was having lunch in the teahouse, and Baian

and Hikojiro ate in a neighboring establishment.

It was one o'clock before Mineyama reappeared. He made his way over the Yodo River toward Fushimi.

"It looks as if he's going to Kyoto," Baian said.

It was only about four miles from the Hachiman Shrine to Fushimi, which was the western gateway to Kyoto. In those days Fushimi was a prosperous port city, and a steady traffic of ships sailed down the Yodo River bound for Osaka. Fushimi had originally sprung up around the castle of a powerful warlord, Toyotomi Hideyoshi, who had united the country after years of civil war. Its origins as a castle town could still be seen in the scale of the streets. But now the city's main claim to fame was its bustling pleasure quarter.

Mineyama walked straight through the city center and out the northern gate, continuing until he arrived at the Gonjoji Temple.

Baian watched as Mineyama entered the temple. Etsudo, Baian's teacher and benefactor, was buried in the Gonjoji's cemetery.

Etsudo had raised Baian from childhood, acting more like a father than a teacher. After his teacher's death Baian had arranged for his burial at the Etsudo family temple. He had returned several times over the years to visit the grave, becoming quite friendly with the priests.

"I'm sorry, Hiko, but I must ask you to wait for me here," Baian said, indicating a small teahouse by the front gate. "Stay here until I get back."

"But…"

"Just leave this to me."

Something about Baian's expression showed that he would not take no for an answer. Hikojiro took a deep breath, then nodded in agreement.

The sun was dropping as Baian walked through the cemetery gateway, but as he approached his teacher's grave the color drained from his face.

He almost doubted his own eyes: Mineyama was kneeling before Etsudo's grave, his hands together in prayer, his eyes closed. Baian hid behind a tree when a temple servant who knew him walked through the cemetery carrying flowers and incense for another grave.

The only movement in the graveyard was the fluttering of a butterfly.

Of course the grave contained not only Etsudo's ashes, but also those of his wife, parents, and grandparents. Mineyama might not have known Etsudo personally. He could have come to pay his respects to one of the doctor's relatives.

After the servant was out of sight, Baian walked quietly up behind the bowed figure. Mineyama turned, and Baian bowed to him politely.

"My name is Fujieda Baian. I am Etsudo's former apprentice; may I ask who you are?" he asked in a low voice.

The samurai hurriedly got to his feet. "My name is Mineyama Matajuro, a retainer of Lord Matsudaira of Wakayama." He replied no less politely.

The minute he heard the samurai speak, Baian knew that this could not be the man who had caused Hikojiro's wife's death. While Hikojiro was obviously not lying, somehow he had made a terrible mistake. Baian was absolutely convinced that the man standing in front of him could never have done the things that Hikojiro had described.

Hikojiro looked on in amazement as the two men walked out of the temple together, talking as they went. As they passed the teahouse, Baian glanced toward his partner and dropped something on the road behind him.

Hikojiro rushed into the street and picked up a tightly folded sheet of paper. He opened it to find a message for him:

> *Follow me and check into the same inn tonight. Something has happened that changes everything.*

Mineyama's story

"My father was a master of the Ittoryu style of swordsmanship and ran a small school in Osaka," Mineyama told Baian while they stood in front of Etsudo's grave. "When I was fourteen and my brother Soichi was still only about twelve, my father became very sick. An oil merchant we were friendly with in Osaka introduced us to Dr. Etsudo, and as a result my father was able to make a full recovery. My father always said that Dr. Etsudo was a brilliant acupuncturist, and that he owed him his life."

Baian realized that this must have been about two years before Etsudo had adopted him, but he had a vague recollection of a *ronin* who used to visit his master about once a year. The man's visits continued for about five years and then suddenly stopped. Baian had not thought about him since, but now he realized that the man must have been Mineyama's father.

That was all he learned standing in front of the grave, but he wanted to know much more. Mineyama had mentioned a brother who was two years younger, and being brothers the chances were that they looked alike. Baian began to suspect that it must have been Mineyama's brother who had raped Hikojiro's wife.

Intent on finding out the truth, Baian took out a sheet of paper and quickly wrote the note for Hikojiro while Mineyama went to pay his respects to the priests.

He had first heard about Etsudo's death six years earlier,

Mineyama told Baian, while visiting Kyoto on business. He had decided to visit the old doctor to pay his respects, but the people in the neighborhood told him that Etsudo had died and gave him directions to the temple where he was buried.

When asked about his father, Mineyama merely replied without elaboration that he was dead.

"I'm on my way to Kyoto myself. Perhaps we could travel together. If I'm not intruding, that is. I'd appreciate the company," Baian said. Mineyama did not seem eager to accept at first. "Of course, if it's at all inconvenient…"

Mineyama appeared to change his mind. "No, of course not," he said. "Let's go together, and you can tell me about Dr. Etsudo on the way."

❖ ❖ ❖

Thus Baian and Mineyama became traveling companions, while Hikojiro trailed along behind them. About eight miles separated Fushimi and Kyoto, and night was deepening by the time they reached the city. Mineyama had booked an inn north of the Gojo Bridge. When they got to the south side of the bridge Baian took his leave.

"I'll be staying near here, but if the opportunity arises, I hope that we'll meet again," Baian said.

"You say you live in Edo?" Mineyama asked.

"Yes."

"Which part?"

"I tend to move around."

Mineyama did not suggest that they meet again in Kyoto.

Baian accompanied Mineyama until he entered the inn, then went back to meet Hikojiro.

"What on earth is going on?"

"I'll explain later."

They registered at the inn next to Mineyama's. After a bath they settled down to their evening meal. Once the waitress had left them alone, Baian said to Hikojiro, "You'll never guess what I learned this afternoon."

"Well?"

"Mineyama has a younger brother."

"What?" Hikojiro could not hide his surprise.

"I think that it must be his brother you're after."

"And where is this bastard brother of his?"

"That's the problem."

"What do you mean?"

"Well, every time I tried to bring the conversation around to his brother, he would change the subject. I'm sure that there is more to this than meets the eye."

After Mineyama's father died, the same merchant who had introduced Etsudo to his father arranged for Mineyama to be adopted by a retainer of Lord Matsudaira. The retainer was only a minor official of his clan, but all the same it was very unusual in those days for a samurai of any rank to adopt the son of a *ronin* as his heir. It reflected very well on the character of Mineyama's father. However, Baian had not managed to find out what had happened to the younger brother, Soichi, or what kind of man he had become.

After finishing their evening meal, Baian suggested that they go out for a walk. They strolled through the inn's garden and discovered that they could see the windows of the upstairs rooms of Mineyama's inn. A light shone in one of the rooms.

The evening breeze had dropped and the night was unnaturally calm.

Baian tugged Hikojiro's sleeve and pointed toward the

lighted window. They hid behind one of the bushes in the garden.

The evening was hot and humid, and the paper screens on the windows were open. As fate would have it, who should look out but Mineyama himself. He was talking, but they could not see his companion.

Baian and Hikojiro exchanged glances. Mineyama had booked into the inn on his own, so this could only mean that he had a visitor.

The samurai disappeared from the window to be replaced a short while later by another man whose profile was lit by the lantern in the room. Baian barely managed to stifle a cry of surprise when he saw the second man.

He looked like a fat middle-aged merchant, but Baian recognized him at once. After looking around the garden, the man closed the screens.

"Did you see him, Hiko?"

"Yes, but what are you so excited about?"

"He once hired me to kill someone."

"What?"

"Yes, it was five years ago now."

Kikuemon's Offer

Five years earlier Baian had already made a name for himself in the underworld as a hired killer. He had come to Kyoto for about six months to visit a friend of his old teacher. While he was there somebody approached him with a contract for a murder. The go-between on that occasion was the man he had just seen in the room with Mineyama.

His name was Kikuemon, and he owned a large restaurant in Osaka. He was also a powerful gang boss who controlled the main pleasure quarters of the city, although this was unknown to most people. He was so powerful that even the city magistrates were scared to cross him. His mistress ran a restaurant in the geisha quarter of Gion.

From time to time he would arrange to have people killed. He accepted only large jobs, and the sums of money involved were huge. It was also said, however, that he would accept contracts only if he felt that society would benefit from the victim's death. He had several assassins whom he used regularly, but five years earlier he had been approached with an urgent job and none of them had been available. He had gone to another boss and asked him to introduce him to one of his men.

"You're in luck," the man replied. "I happen to know of a very good man who is in Kyoto at the moment."

That was how he came to meet Baian. He paid him fifty pieces of gold to kill the retainer of a court noble, and Baian did so with a single needle. Kikuemon had been highly impressed and praised his work.

"If you're free, I'd like you to work for me full time. I'll make it worth your while." Kikuemon treated him well, and Baian would never forget his kindness.

But what was he doing in the room with Mineyama? Hikojiro had no idea either.

"I think we can at least be sure that Mineyama will be staying the night at the inn next door, so why don't we get back to our room and think about it over a drink."

"But what are we going to do?"

"That's the question." Baian drank a cup of *sake*, then made up his mind. "Wait here. I'm going out for a while."

"But where are you going at this time of night?"

"To Gion. I'm sure Kikuemon will be staying at his mistress's restaurant."

"Are you going to see him?"

"Yes. Keep your eye on Mineyama, will you?"

"Leave it to me."

"Give the maid a tip and see if she can move us into one of the rooms on the second floor. Try to get one that looks into Mineyama's."

Baian left the inn and headed toward the Gion pleasure quarter.

❖ ❖ ❖

"I was in town, so I thought I would drop by and pay my respects. Is the boss keeping well?" Baian said when he arrived at the restaurant. Realizing who he was, Kikuemon's mistress came out to greet him in person.

"Dr. Baian, this is a surprise. You're in luck, the boss is in Kyoto tonight."

"You mean he's here?" Baian said, feigning surprise.

"Yes, I know he'll be delighted to see you," she said and virtually dragged him into the building and to the suite of rooms Kikuemon always occupied when he stayed in Kyoto. Five years earlier Baian had used his acupuncture to cure Kikuemon's mistress, and she had held him in the greatest esteem ever since.

"Now, this is a surprise," Kikuemon said as Baian entered the room. "Osaki, get our guest something to eat."

She hurried back with *sake*, having ordered the kitchen to prepare a lavish meal. The three of them ate while they chatted.

"And what brings you to Kyoto this time?"

"Oh, nothing really. I had some time on my hands, so I thought I'd come and visit Dr. Etsudo's grave."

"It's good to meet a man who respects his elders, but you say that you have nothing on at the moment?"

"That's right, I'm quite free," Baian replied with a smile.

"But I might be open to offers if you need something done."

"What?" Kikuemon gave an embarrassed bow. "I should have guessed I couldn't fool you."

"What is it? Is it a difficult job?"

"Yes, but I don't think it would interest you."

"Well, tell me about it anyway."

"The man I have been asked to dispose of is evil incarnate; he causes nothing but misery, and the sooner he's dealt with, the better. The only problem is that though it's going to be a tricky job, I can't pay very much to have it done."

"Is he that dangerous then?"

"Yes, very, but the money is…I know that I can trust you, so I'll be quite frank. Usually I wouldn't accept a job this cheap, but it was brought to me by a very old merchant friend and I didn't have the heart to send him away."

"And it's this merchant who wants the job done?"

"No, not exactly. The man who wants the job done is a samurai, a retainer of an important lord. He cannot let it be known that he is involved. Unfortunately, however, this samurai would be no match for the person he wants to have killed, and so he had no option but to come to me."

"Go on."

"The samurai is not a rich man, so I'm afraid there is very little money involved. I cannot pay the assassin who takes it on more than twenty gold pieces."

"I don't mind, you've got me quite interested."

"You mean you'll do it?"

"Yes."

Kikuemon gave a wry grin. "You're a strange one."

Baian stayed at the restaurant for about two hours discussing the job. As the fee was so small, Kikuemon decided to tell Baian the whole story.

❖ ❖ ❖

When Baian returned to the inn, he found Hikojiro waiting for him impatiently. He had moved to the second-floor from which he could look directly into Mineyama's room.

"I suppose Mineyama has already gone to sleep."

"Yes. What did you manage to find out?"

"It's lucky we didn't kill him before we found out more. It wasn't Mineyama who raped your wife, but his brother, Soichi."

"What?" Hikojiro's face turned pale, and he broke into a cold sweat.

"You won't believe this," Baian said.

"What?"

"Mineyama came here all the way from Wakayama with the sole aim of asking Kikuemon to have his brother murdered."

"You're not serious."

"He is acting through an intermediary, a merchant who was a very close friend of his father, and who had arranged for his adoption by a samurai family in Wakayama."

Kikuemon would never accept a contract on the word of an intermediary alone. He always insisted on meeting the person who actually wanted the job done and discussing it in detail before making his decision. He had been known to turn down a job after having talked it over with the client, and that was why he had a good name among professional killers.

"Soichi is in Kyoto at the moment. He's like a poisonous snake; there's no good in him at all. Even his brother cannot ignore him any longer and has been forced to act, but you'll never believe this," Baian said slapping Hikojiro on the back. "I accepted the contract to kill him from Kikuemon. I'm afraid that it's only worth twenty gold pieces, but all the same, I'd appreciate it if you could give me a hand with the job."

A Tale of Two Brothers

The village of Yamabana lay to the north of Kyoto on the Wakasa Road. Because the capital was a long way from the sea, all the fish that was eaten there was carried down this road. Yamabana had two or three restaurants that catered to gourmets who came just to eat fresh fish.

Immediately west of Yamabana, across the Takano River, was the small hamlet of Matsugasaki. Mineyama's brother, Soichi, was living there in an abandoned farmhouse.

Unlike his brother, Soichi took after their father in prowess at arms. He had been a skilled swordsman since childhood, and by the time he was sixteen none of the students in his father's school could beat him.

"There lies the root of the problem," Mineyama told Kikuemon. "They say that overconfidence in a young man will lead to no good, and it's true."

After Mineyama went to Wakayama, Soichi took over the management of their father's school. He seemed to be doing very well at first. The problems started later. Still only twenty, he was so overbearing that he drove away all his students. The school went bankrupt, and he began to spend all his time drinking and whoring. In order to get money, he turned to crime. This went on for some time until one day he fought a duel with a samurai and killed him. Forced to leave Osaka, he set out on the road. Some time later he turned up in Edo with another *ronin*. It was then that he raped Hikojiro's wife.

117

Mineyama was not worried as long as Soichi was far away, but every now and again, he would appear in Wakayama to demand money. Mineyama was only an adopted son, and his new family was by no means wealthy, so these visits caused him a good deal of grief.

Two years earlier Soichi had moved to Kyoto. The furor over the duel in Osaka had died down, and, unlike the police in Edo or Osaka, the authorities in Kyoto were largely ineffectual. Kyoto was the home of the imperial court, and its citizens were generally law abiding. The chief magistrate tended to avoid confrontations, so someone like Soichi could do almost anything he pleased.

He had come in the company of his old friend, a *ronin* from Edo named Kimura, and four other no-good *ronin* he had met on his travels. They came across an empty farmhouse in Matsugasaki and moved in without asking permission. The villagers tried to drive them away, but they would not move; in fact they often raided the surrounding houses to steal food and rape the women.

The villagers complained to the authorities, and the constables were sent to sort it out, but when they saw who they had to deal with, they beat a hasty retreat.

After this, Soichi often appeared in Kyoto, eating in restaurants without paying, stealing, and extorting money from merchants. He had lived this way for more than twenty years now and was an expert at it. The magistrates could never find any evidence against him because his victims were all too frightened to testify.

One day the merchant who had arranged for Mineyama's adoption was in Kyoto on business. When he heard about Soichi's criminal exploits, he became very upset and hurried to Wakayama to tell Mineyama what was going on.

"If word gets out that he's your brother, it will make your

position here untenable. You'll have to deal with him somehow."

Mineyama realized that he had no choice, but there was nothing he himself could do about Soichi. He had never been interested in swordsmanship or the other martial arts, preferring to devote himself to reading and study.

"I suppose I should put an end to him myself, but I don't know if I'm capable. All the same, I can't allow him to continue behaving as he does."

He was desperate, but then the merchant whispered into his ear, "I know that it's not my position to interfere, but maybe it would be best if you were to pay someone else to remove the root of your problem."

"Someone else?"

"Leave it to me."

The merchant had gone to Kikuemon to see what could be done, and though Kikuemon agreed that it was possible, he said that it would be extremely difficult to find a man to do it for less than one hundred fifty gold pieces.

Neither the merchant nor Mineyama could come up with such a huge sum of money. They both tried everything possible to raise the money, but in the end they managed to collect only forty-five gold pieces, and this is what Mineyama took with him when he went to see Kikuemon in Kyoto.

❖ ❖ ❖

"This is not going to be an easy job, you know," Baian reported to Hikojiro after checking out the house. "There are six *ronin* we have to get rid of, and they're all dangerous. We'll have to give it a lot of thought because we're no match for them man to man."

Hikojiro replied with a careless laugh, "Don't be such a

coward! If we both put our minds to it, we're sure to come up with something."

"All right, just don't get carried away."

"Don't worry, I'm quite happy to spend as much time as it takes."

As soon as Mineyama received confirmation from Kikue-mon that the job would be done, he returned to Wakayama and waited.

Whittling Down the Opposition

That afternoon, two of the *ronin* who were living with Soi-chi were walking through the crowds in Shijo Street by the Kamo River. They were both young and very drunk. Their eyes had the same bestial look as Soichi's when he had raped Hikojiro's wife twenty years earlier, but the cut of their clothes showed that they were making a good living in Kyoto.

This stretch of Shijo Street was one of the most popular areas in the whole city, and on a sunny autumn day it was packed with people and stalls.

"Get out of the way!"

"Where do you think you're going?" the *ronin* shouted at the passersby.

They crossed the bridge, acting as if they owned it, push-ing people out of their way and slapping them if they were too slow to move.

Suddenly Baian and Hikojiro appeared on the opposite side of the bridge and started to hurry toward the *ronin*. As they passed at the middle of the bridge, they purposely jostled them.

"Fool!" roared one *ronin*.

"You'll pay for that!" the other raged.

The two swordsmen raised their fists, about to hit Baian and Hikojiro, but all of a sudden both *ronin* suddenly froze.

Their eyes rolled up to show the whites.

"What's wrong with them?" a man asked.

"Are they sick?"

The people on the bridge stared at the two *ronin* in amazement, but by then there was no sign of Hikojiro or Baian, who had plunged needles into the men's hearts as they walked past.

The two men staggered a few paces, then collapsed face down onto the planks of the bridge.

When the police finally arrived, they moved the bodies away but did little else. It was easy to see what kind of men they were, and the authorities did not even bother to find out if anyone might want to claim the bodies.

A few days passed without their returning to the house in Matsugasaki, but Soichi simply assumed that they had tired of their life with him and moved on elsewhere. A short while later, however, one of the other young *ronin* in Soichi's band returned from Kyoto with news of the missing men.

"They say that two *ronin* were involved in a fight on the Shijo Bridge, and both were killed. You don't suppose it could have been them?" the young man asked.

"Could be," Soichi replied, showing little concern. "Don't worry about it, they brought it on themselves. Neither of them was very good with a sword, but they were always throwing their weight around. I'm surprised it didn't happen earlier."

There were now only four *ronin* left in the house.

Another week went by. One day Soichi called in the two younger men.

"I want you to go down to the Heishichi in Yamabana and get me fish and *sake*. If the owner makes a fuss, break his arm. That'll give him something to think about."

The two men walked out into the rain.

The Heishichi was a nearby inn they terrorized regularly. They stole food and *sake,* and if the proprietor dared to complain, they beat up the customers.

After the two *ronin* left, Soichi lay down on some of the bedding that was strewn over the floor and turned to Kimura, the man he had been traveling with for the past twenty years.

"You know, Kimura," he said, "I think it's time we moved on."

They were now both in their forties.

"Yes, I guess you're right. We've managed to get away with a lot so far, but it can't go on indefinitely."

"Why don't we go down and visit my brother in Wakayama again? I just love the look on his face when we arrive. He's always good for money, even though it isn't much."

"We'd better get some real money before we leave, though."

"Right, leave it to me," Soichi said with a grin.

While they were talking, the two younger *ronin* were approaching the bridge over the Takano River. It was a simple affair: a few planks lashed together across the river.

Two farmers crossed from the opposite side and walked toward them.

"Excuse me," one of them said, bowing low.

They wore wide-brimmed hats and straw coats for protection from the rain. One of the *ronin* carried an umbrella over his shoulder, and he lifted it threateningly, his eyes flashing with anger.

"You rude little bastard, remove your hat when addressing your betters."

The farmers made no move to comply, but looked up at the *ronin.* Suddenly a loud hiss sounded. The two *ronin* put their hands to their faces, attempting to fend off the darts that were being fired at them, but they struck their eyes and throats. In the next instant Baian and Hikojiro reached out, covered their mouths, and with their free hands, stabbed them in the heart.

The two *ronin* died instantly. Baian and Hikojiro buried the bodies in the woods. The blood that had covered the road was soon washed away by the rain.

That evening Soichi turned to Kimura. Although it was dark, they had not bothered to light a lantern.

"They're late."

"Maybe they ran off."

"Do you think so?"

"It's because you treat them so badly."

"But at least I make sure they don't want for *sake* or women. I even give them spending money. When I first met them, they didn't know where their next meal was coming from. I don't see what they've got to complain about."

"Anyway, it looks as if it's just you and me again."

"To tell the truth, it's a relief to be rid of them at last." But his voice sounded strangely sad and wistful.

Even when they relaxed in the house, their swords never left their sides—a reflection of the sort of lives they had followed all these years. Baian and Hikojiro spied on the two *ronin* often. They quickly realized that they would not be as easy to kill as the other four had been. But though they were never off their guard even for a moment, in the end it would not save them. The instant Hikojiro had laid eyes on them, he was certain that these were the two men who had ruined his life twenty years earlier.

Hikojiro's Revenge

Three days passed, and it was still raining. But rather

than the heavy rain that fell on the day that the two younger *ronin* died, this was a light misty rain that had continued since morning. Two naked women were in the house—servant girls from the Heishichi.

That afternoon Soichi turned to his partner and said, "It's still raining. How about looking for a bit of company?"

They barged into the restaurant and grabbed the first young women they met. Knocking them unconscious, they carried them back to the house. The owner of the restaurant witnessed it all, but he could do nothing to stop them.

When they got back to the house they drank the stolen *sake* and then began to have their way with the women. But what they did to their victims went far beyond rape. The two *ronin* had experienced so many horrors during their lives that they thought nothing of inflicting pain. Their repertory of perversion was endless.

Kimura sometimes said he could feel the doors of hell opening for him, which showed the depth of his fear and uncertainty. Only when they were inflicting pain on women did they manage to escape their fear for a short while.

The girls could not defend themselves. Their clothes were ripped off, and so merciless was their beating that after an hour they were hardly conscious of what was being done to them. Their bodies were soaked with sweat and their naked breasts were streaked with blood where the men had torn at their flesh with their teeth.

"Come on, bitch, your heart isn't in it any more!" Soichi screamed, and drawing his short sword, he cut off the girl's hair. She was so overcome by what had been done to her, however, that she could not even cry out.

The flickering light of the lantern made the room look like a cave or animal's lair, and it was filled with the smell of sex and sweat. Kimura had exhausted himself and was dozing with his head resting on the girl's naked lap.

"You fucking bitch!" Soichi shouted at the prostrate figure beneath him. He grasped a handful of her pubic hair and started to tear it out. The girl screamed and tried to get away, but he hit her in the face. Then climbing on her back, he started to ride her like a horse.

"Damn you! Damn you!" He gave a cracked laugh then returned to tearing the woman's pubic hair. The girl fainted, blood spreading over her stomach and thighs.

Eventually Soichi tired of the sport and went to the kitchen to get a drink of water. He picked up the ladle of the water butt and drank it dry several times. Kimura staggered toward him.

"After all the *sake*, I could do with some water, too," he said.

"It tastes real good."

"I'm beat."

Kimura drank several ladlefuls. Both men carried their short swords, the habits of a lifetime never deserting them even when they seemed unnecessary.

"What are we going to do with the women?"

"Leave them where they are, we can use them again tomorrow."

They kicked the girls over to one side of the room and then flopped down on their beds.

A little while passed.

"Soichi!" Kimura cried suddenly, sitting up. "I feel sick. How do you feel?"

"Wha—what's the matter?"

"Ah! My chest…it hurts." He cried out, clutching at his chest wildly.

"What's wrong? Are you all right?"

"No, it's…Aaah! I can't stand it."

"Kimura!" Soichi's face was tense with fear. Suddenly he felt a pain in his own chest, a pain like red hot needles being driven into his heart.

They rolled on the floor in agony, coughing up large amounts of blood until they both grew still. Baian and Hikojiro watched the whole scene through a hole in the farmhouse wall.

"Things worked out well, didn't they, Hiko?"

"Yes, they never suspected the water had been poisoned when they were out getting their *sake* and women. They were even kind enough to drink a lot to make sure the poison would kill them."

"Yes, we were very lucky. I never dreamed that they would both have a drink at the same time. I thought we'd have to think up something else to get the last one."

They walked through the wet night without a lantern to guide them.

"But what if those women had tried to drink the water?" Hikojiro asked.

"No need to worry," Baian replied, showing him a length of fine rope that he carried. "I wrapped this around the pail, and if either of the women had tried to drink, I would have tipped it over. I tipped it over anyway after the poison started to take effect."

"You think of everything, Baian," Hikojiro said with a note of admiration in his voice.

"But that poison was expensive. I had to spend everything we were given for the job."

Hikojiro did not reply and, as they walked, Baian realized that he was crying.

When they got back to their inn, Hikojiro knelt on the floor and bowed to Baian.

That night the rain finally stopped.

"What do you say, Hikojiro, shall we start heading back to Edo soon?" asked Baian.

"I'll leave it entirely up to you."

They sat and drank *sake*, eating some of the pickled eggplant that the waitress had left them for the night.

"This sure is good," Hikojiro remarked, licking his lips.

"I read in a book that fall eggplants cool the intestines and are poisonous."

"You know too much for your own good, Baian."

"No, seriously. They're just so good that people can't stop themselves from overeating, and anything is bad in excess."

"Like those two *ronin*, they certainly drank to excess, didn't they? And look what happened to them!"

He lay down, still laughing, and within minutes started to snore. As a rule he never fell asleep so easily. Baian stood up and covered his friend with a quilt.

❖ ❖ ❖

One autumn day two years later, Baian was approached by a middle-aged samurai. Looking closely, he realized that it was Mineyama. He had come to Edo on business and had put on so much weight that Baian had not recognized him.

"Why don't we talk over a few cups of *sake*?" Baian said, leading the way to a nearby tavern. They chatted for some time until Baian casually said, "You mentioned last time we met that you had a brother. I've always wanted a brother myself, being an only child."

Mineyama interrupted him with a wave of his hand. "No, you're wrong. You're much better off without any brothers," he said with a scowl.

"Really?"

"Yes, really."

"By the way, how is your brother? I trust that he's keeping well?"

"No," he said, a smile of perfect satisfaction spreading over his face. "He died some time ago."

LEAVE HIM TO HIS FATE

Two weeks had passed since Baian and Hikojiro had killed the *ronin* Soichi and his five henchmen, but they still showed no sign of leaving Kyoto. The authorities had not bothered to investigate the deaths of the six *ronin*. They had caused so much trouble in Kyoto that nobody cared who had killed them; people were just relieved to know they were dead. In any case, Baian and Hikojiro were in the clear. Even if there had been an investigation, nothing linked them to the murders.

Summer had turned to fall. The scenery of the ancient capital improved by the day as the trees decked themselves in autumn colors. Baian and Hikojiro enjoyed visiting the sights around the city, especially Hikojiro, who was seeing them for the first time. They had almost managed to forget that they were hired killers, until Hikojiro suggested that they had better start thinking of returning to Edo.

"I want to visit Ohiro's grave," he said, "to tell her that I've avenged her at last."

Baian counted the money they had left.

"At this rate, we'll have to start work the minute we get home. We've got very little to spare."

"I know," Hikojiro replied with a sigh of resignation.

At that point a man came in to tell Baian that Kikuemon wanted to see him at the Izutsu restaurant.

❖ ❖ ❖

"I feel guilty about having given you such a cheap job," Kikuemon said to Baian. "I'd like to make up for it by offering you another one. This one will pay very well. When were you planning to return to Edo?"

"Well," Baian said, his eyes twinkling with laughter, "I've run out of money now, so I'll have to work as a doctor here for a while to raise the money for the trip."

"I heard from Osaki that you were still in town, so I sent for you straight away," Kikuemon explained. "The money's good, but it won't be an easy job."

"How much is it worth?"

"One hundred gold pieces."

The price for killing varied with the identity of the target, but fifty pieces of gold was generally considered to be a good price. To be worth one hundred, the victim must be a very special man indeed. Baian remained silent. It was not his place to ask for the reasons why the victim deserved to die, that was the responsibility of the go-between who offered the job. He trusted Kikuemon implicitly. He had worked for him three times in the past, and his trust had not been betrayed. He made up his mind.

"Very well, I'll do it."

"Good."

"Tell me about it."

"To tell the truth, I am offering this one to you after seeing the way you and Hikojiro dealt with those *ronin*. I don't think you'll be able to manage this one on your own."

"Who is it? Where does he live?"

"His name is Kaneko Matazo. He's a *ronin* and a formidable swordsman."

"And I just have to kill this one *ronin*, do I?"

"Yes. Are you sure you want to take it on?"

Baian felt his enthusiasm for the job growing. If Kaneko were as strong and evil as Kikuemon said, it would be a challenge to pit his wits against his strength.

"And where does he live?"

"In a village a little way out of Kyoto."

Steamed Mushrooms

Insects chirped in the garden of the inn as Baian and Hikojiro sat drinking. The aroma of steamed mushrooms filled the room.

"That smells real good, Baian," Hikojiro said, smacking his lips.

Baian reached to pick up one of the mushrooms with his chopsticks, handing it to Hikojiro.

"They taste even better if they're cooked as soon as they're picked," Baian explained.

"To get back to the Kaneko job," Hikojiro said. "We're both exhausted after dealing with those *ronin,* and we've got enough money to get us back to Edo without hardship. Are you sure you're not taking on too much?"

"I know, Hiko, but it's a hundred gold pieces we're talking about here."

"Yes, it's not often you get an offer like that," Hikojiro agreed.

"Why don't we do it together? We can make fifty gold pieces each and then take our time going home."

Hikojiro nodded his agreement. "I leave it entirely up to you."

"You can't do that."

"No, I've decided that from now on I'll do anything you say."

Baian did not push the subject.

"So we'll do it together, then."

"That's fine by me."

Their eyes met for a minute.

"It'll be all right this time," they said in unison. The sixth sense that all hired killers possessed told them that they would finish the job without mishap—but they both knew that this sense was not infallible.

After Baian had helped him avenge his wife and child, Hikojiro had decided that there was nothing he would not do for his friend, even if it cost him his life.

"So where do we find this Kaneko character?"

"In a village called Mekawa, a little way from Kusatsu. Apparently he's hiding together with a youth of fifteen or sixteen."

"Hiding?"

"Kikuemon didn't give me the details, but he did tell me that Kaneko had been the retainer of a lord in the west of the country."

"Is the young man his son or brother?"

"I don't know."

"Are we killing Kaneko for his former lord?"

"Kikuemon didn't say and I wasn't about to ask." Baian pursed his lips and took out his pipe, which he kept in a case suspended from the back of his sash. The solid silver pipe was made by one of the best pipemakers in the country. He kept it as a memento of his teacher and benefactor, Etsudo.

"This Kaneko has been attacked six times by swordsmen, and each time he killed his attackers."

"He sounds a worthy opponent," Hikojiro said grimly.

"Not only that but he's a huge man."

"In that case, maybe you ought to challenge him to a bout of sumo."

Baian took the fifty coins he had received as an advance payment, counted out twenty-five of them, and placed them in front of Hikojiro. Then he blew a stream of smoke from his mouth.

"When are we leaving?" Hikojiro asked. "Tomorrow?"

Baian nodded.

It was just over six leagues from Kyoto to Kusatsu, and from there only a short distance to the village of Mekawa. They decided to find an inn in Kusatsu first and use that as a base from which to spy on their prey. Baian took out the map Kikuemon had given him and spread it for Hikojiro to see. It was a street plan of Mekawa, and the house in which Kaneko was hiding was clearly marked.

A Stroke of Luck

Kusatsu was an important weighing station to the east of Kyoto, where the two main highways linking Edo and the capital divided. Its many inns and taverns catered to an unending stream of travelers and merchants.

Baian and Hikojiro left Kyoto wearing light traveling clothes. When they arrived in Kusatsu, they booked into an inn called the Nomuraya. The first night they stayed there, Baian tipped the staff generously and became very friendly with them, because he intended to use the inn as a base until they managed to complete the job.

"We're waiting for some friends to join us here," Baian explained to the landlord. "So we'll be staying for a few days."

Late next morning Baian and Hikojiro, wearing ordinary townsmen's clothes, set out for Mekawa. Baian was playing the part of a doctor from Kyoto, and Hikojiro pretended to be his servant.

"We'll be visiting a friend in Ishibe," Baian said as he left the inn. "We shouldn't be late back."

Ishibe was about two and a half leagues away, and Mekawa was on the way. It was not much of a village, but it boasted an inn called the Iseya, which served a famous speciality.

When they arrived in Mekawa, they were a bit early for lunch, but Baian pointed out the Iseya and said, "Did you know that this is where grilled tofu in sweet bean sauce was first made?"

"You know everything, Baian."

They went in and tried some of the tofu, washed down with a flask of *sake*. Because it was still early they were the only customers.

There was no wind, and the sky was overcast.

"That was delicious, and the *sake* was good too," Baian said to the waitress with a smile as he tipped her. "I believe a big *ronin* is living in the village with a young man. I was told that he was sick, and I've come to examine him. Could you tell me where he lives?"

As soon as he spoke, the waitress's attitude changed. "Wait here a minute, please," she said and rushed into the kitchen, leaving Baian and Hikojiro to exchange bemused looks.

Very soon the elderly owner of the inn came out from the back. "Excuse me, sir, but are you the doctor from Otsu?"

"That's correct," Baian replied without a moment's hesitation.

"One of the young men of the village was sent to fetch you this morning, but he came back saying that he hadn't been able to talk to you. You are Dr. Kyoan, I take it?"

"That's correct."

The owner apparently knew Kaneko well, and, moreover, either the *ronin* or his young companion was sick. The lie that Baian had told had turned out to be the truth. It was an unbelievable stroke of luck.

"Is he very bad?"

"Yes, he is," the landlord said with a disapproving look, obviously shocked that a doctor should have been sitting around eating and drinking when he had a patient waiting. It seemed that though Kaneko had been living here only for three months he was popular in the village.

"Well, let's go and see the patient," Baian said, rising to his feet and giving Hikojiro a knowing look.

The waitress led the way through the field behind the inn to a house nestled in a bamboo grove at the foot of a hill.

"He's in there," she said, pointing at the house.

Baian gave Hikojiro a look as if to say "This is it, one way or another." Hikojiro furtively started to prepare his blowpipe as he walked.

When they entered the darkened house, the first thing they saw was a huge man writhing in agony on a bed in the corner. Sitting next to him was a boy of fifteen or sixteen who seemed to be at a loss as to what to do. The giant was obviously in terrible pain.

The boy rushed over. "Dr. Kyoan?" he asked.

"Yes," Baian replied coolly.

"Quickly, see what you can do for him!"

Kaneko's Fate

The man lying in the bed looked immensely strong. The Satsuma-style mounted sword lying next to him was so long that it looked impossibly heavy for an ordinary man to wield.

This was the *ronin* Kaneko.

Although the pain was bad enough to make him writhe and groan, it seemed to have eased a little for the time being.

"My name is Kyuma," the young man said. He was obviously beside himself with worry, but he spoke in a calm, measured tone. "Two or three times this morning he's had these terrible fits and thrown himself out of bed. I and two lads from the village did our best to hold him down, but he was too strong for us."

Baian found it difficult to believe that Kaneko was the evil man that Kikuemon had depicted. He gave Kaneko a quick examination, and, being a skilled doctor, he did a much better job than any country doctor would have done. Kyuma sat looking on, clenching his fists in an attempt to stop himself from trembling. Two well-built farmhands sat behind him. They were obviously there to hold Kaneko down when he had his fits. Both looked exhausted.

Kaneko's huge frame was covered with thick black hair. There was a sword cut on his shoulder and two more on his chest. The wounds were shallow and apparently fresh.

Baian guessed that the wounds must have been inflicted during the previous murder attempts, but it would take a very skilled swordsman indeed to better this huge man. That was why Kikuemon had come to professional killers like himself and Hikojiro to do the job. Although they had no skill at all with swords, they knew countless other ways of dealing with a foe—needles, blowpipes, poisons—and most of all, they had the will to succeed.

"And this person is your… ?" Baian asked, looking up at Kyuma.

"My…friend," the boy replied, the soft skin of his neck flushing red.

"Your friend?"

"Yes."

The powerfully built Kaneko was about thirty, while Kyuma was a delicate-looking boy at least fifteen years his junior. Baian found it difficult to believe that they were just friends.

Baian finished his examination and indicated to Kyuma that they should step outside.

"How is he, doctor?"

Baian shook his head.

"Isn't there anything you can do for him?"

"I'm afraid that he is beyond medical care."

Kaneko was suffering from appendicitis, a condition that can be cured today with a simple operation, but in those days nothing could be done except to wait and pray.

At that moment Kaneko let out a terrible cry. Kyuma rushed back indoors. Hikojiro had followed them out and now moved to stand by Baian.

"We're not needed here," Baian said.

"How long does he have?"

"He probably won't last out the day."

"Nothing like this has ever happened to me. I'm con-tracted to kill a man only to find that he's already dying when I get there."

"Me too."

The sound that issued from the inside of the house was more like the cry of a beast in pain than of a man.

"Aahhh! My guts are going to burst!" Kaneko screamed.

His convulsions became more violent. Kyuma and the two farmhands could do nothing but try to hold him down.

"I can't stand it any longer! I can't stand the pain! Kyuma, you'll have to manage on your own…this is the end!"

He suddenly got to his feet, shaking the three boys loose like flies.

"Wait! Kaneko, don't!"

Hearing the pain in Kyuma's voice, Baian and Hikojiro ran back into the house. They were amazed by what they saw. The three young men were still lying on the floor where they had fallen. Kaneko was standing, his legs apart, his hand on the hilt of his short sword. He drew the blade and plunged it into his heart, spraying the room with blood.

Baian stood rooted to the spot. Kaneko fell to his knees. His hands released the hilt of the sword, and he fell backward and lay face up.

"Kaneko!" Kyuma screamed, and ran over to bury his face in the huge man's chest.

The two farmhands looked on in silence.

Forbidden Love

"I think Kyuma and Kaneko were lovers," Baian said to Hikojiro.

"That's the impression I got too," Hikojiro replied.

The two had hurried back to their inn and checked out straight away. With Kaneko dead, they had no reason to remain in Kusatsu. That night they planned to stay in Otsu.

"This means we won't be getting a penny after all."

"It can't be helped."

Kaneko had died of natural causes, without their assistance, so they would not receive their payment—they had no right to it.

If Baian were to tell Kikuemon that he had caused Kaneko's death, he could not only keep the advance but also receive the remaining fifty gold pieces. But if the truth ever came out, his reputation would be ruined.

As they crossed the Seta Bridge, Baian turned to Hikojiro. "I said just now that I thought they were lovers, but I don't think it was a sexual relationship."

There are two types of relationship between men: One is sexual, like that between a man and a woman, and the other purely platonic. The latter was very common among samurai during the Edo period, and Baian believed that this was what Kaneko and Kyuma had shared.

"Do you think so?" Hikojiro replied with a wry grin. "I'm over forty now, but I'm afraid that's one thing I'll never be able to understand."

"You know, Hiko…"

"What?"

Dusk was deepening. Baian stood on the crest of the bridge, looking down at the river.

"You know…"

"What are you trying to say, Baian?"

"I don't think that they were bad people."

"I got the same impression."

"I can't help feeling that whoever paid for this job lied to Kikuemon about his true motives."

"I wonder why they were hiding?"

"I don't know."

"Who do you think paid for the job?"

"I have no idea."

"But whoever it was knew where they were hiding, and was probably keeping an eye on the house."

"Which would mean that they saw us too."

"It's the first time anything like this has happened to me."

"Anyway, let's get back to Kyoto," Baian said. "Once we've returned the money to Kikuemon, we can start our trip home."

"Sounds good to me."

"You know, I'm rather looking forward to working as a doctor again and earning some honest money for a change."

"The same goes for me."

After a night in Otsu, they arrived in Kyoto the next morning, going straight to see Kikuemon at his mistress's restaurant.

Before Baian had a chance to say anything, Kikuemon clapped him on the back, and said, "Well done. I knew I could rely on you." Then he added, surprise showing in his voice, "All the same, I never imagined you'd be able to do it so quickly."

Clearly, he had already received a report of Kaneko's death, which meant that he must have had someone watching the *ronin*'s house in Mekawa. Whoever it was must have thought that Kaneko's death was the work of Baian and Hikojiro.

"Well, here is the remainder of the money," Kikuemon said, putting the money on the table.

For a moment Baian said nothing. Hikojiro kept his eyes lowered, a faint smile playing on his lips. Suddenly Baian stretched out his hand and picked up the money.

"Thank you," he said, slipping the purse of coins into his kimono.

Hikojiro was amazed. He gave Baian a look as if to say, What are you doing? If you don't tell the truth now, you'll be finished. But Baian's face remained expressionless.

"The night you gave me the job," Baian began, "we hurried to Mekawa and slipped some poison into Kaneko's *sake*. You'll appreciate that it was very tricky because we had to make sure we killed Kaneko without hurting Kyuma. I must admit, though, things went even better than we dared hope."

They left the restaurant and hurried back to their inn, where they began to pack for their return to Edo.

Hikojiro remained silent.

Baian put on his gloves. "I decided we should take the money after all," he said, looking at Hikojiro out of the corner of his eye.

Hikojiro looked at him in silence for a moment, then said, "It's your decision. I'll go along with whatever you say."

They left Kyoto that same day, and by nightfall they were staying in Otsu again.

A Change of Plan

That night at about eight o'clock Baian went to the toilet, which was next to the inner garden. He was just about to go back to his room when he heard footsteps in the corridor. He guessed that some late arrivals were just on their way back from the bath. One of them said, "Now that Kaneko's dead, we have nothing to worry about."

As soon as Baian heard that, he stayed where he was and waited. As soon as the three samurai had walked past, he crept out and watched them enter a room at the end of the corridor. Then he hurried back to his room on the second floor where Hikojiro was still drinking.

"Hiko, things are beginning to become more interesting."

"Why? What's happened?"

Baian quickly explained what he had overheard.

A few minutes later, Hikojiro crawled under the floor of the room where the three samurai were drinking. He stayed for almost two hours, listening to their conversation, then he left and had another bath to warm himself up before returning to his own room. When Hikojiro came in, Baian started to warm a flask of *sake* for him.

"You won't believe this, Baian."

"What did you hear?"

"Kyuma used to be a page to a lord's son."

"Which lord?"

"I didn't hear, and it doesn't make much difference anyway."

"What else?"

"Well, the young lord tried to force Kyuma to have sex with him, but the boy refused."

Stung by Kyuma's refusal, the young lord decided to punish him by ordering his attendants to smear his face with animal dung.

"The young lord isn't a child anymore," Hikojiro heard one of the samurai say. "There was no reason for him to go that far."

"But it's what they said afterward that's really interesting."

Kyuma could not forgive his master for the way in which he had been treated, and although he looked a child he was very strong willed. He bided his time until it was his turn to be on night duty outside the young lord's room. In the middle of the night he stole into the room, stabbed his master with a dagger, and escaped from the castle.

"So that's why they're after him. What happened to his family?" Baian asked.

"They all died—suicide."

"That means they knew what he planned to do, and they killed themselves in order to allow him to act without hesitation."

From what Hikojiro had managed to piece together

from the samurai's conversation, Kyuma had gotten his revenge. Kaneko must have been a retainer of the same lord, but when he saw what Kyuma had done, he left his master and fled with the boy in order to protect him from the samurai who would be sent to bring him back.

The clan was trying to get Kyuma back to punish him, but they could not act openly, because people would sympathize with Kyuma if they knew why he had killed his master. At the same time, the clan could not allow Kyuma and Kaneko to go unpunished. It had sent several swordsmen after them to kill them, but the swordsmen themselves had all ended up dead. Finally someone had contacted Kikuemon, and that was when Baian and Hikojiro became involved.

"So much for samurai!" Baian said with contempt. "They talk about the Way of the Warrior, but they can't even catch a boy and his lover."

With Kaneko out of the way, it would not be difficult for the clan to capture Kyuma; no doubt the three samurai in the room below had been sent for that purpose. They had probably been ordered to bring him back for punishment, or, if that was impossible, to kill him where he was.

"But Kyuma doesn't seem to be aware that they know about his hiding place," Baian said.

"No, as long as Kaneko was in the house with him, they wouldn't gain anything by letting Kyuma know they were on to him."

"So I was right to take the gold after all."

"You really have a sense for these things, Baian."

"No doubt they told Kikuemon that Kaneko was an evil man who had turned against his master, and he believed them."

"How do you think they got in touch with him?"

"Probably through a merchant in Osaka. Kikuemon has a lot of connections there."

"What do you think, Baian?"

"All right, I know what you're going to say, and I think you're probably right."

"Let's have a drink first."

"Yes, then we can discuss it in detail. What's that?"

"Eh?"

"Oh, it's only the rain."

"By the way, do you think Kyuma will allow those samurai to take him without a fight?"

"No, I would say that he would fight to the end."

"He'll be killed then."

"Yes, it looks that way."

Death Stalks the Night

At two o'clock in the morning Baian and Hikojiro crept into the room of the three samurai, who had all been drinking and were now sound asleep.

The two killers kneeled next to the pillows of the sleeping men. Hikojiro found a pitcher of water and emptied it onto a tray. Then he took out a sheet of paper and soaked it in the water.

Meanwhile, Baian slipped a leather ring onto his finger, removed a needle from the inside of his collar, and held it between his teeth. He nodded to Hikojiro that he was ready.

Hikojiro picked up the sheet of wet paper and plastered it over the face of the closest of the three sleeping samurai. Immediately, Baian imbedded his assassin's needle deep into the samurai's ear. The man twitched, then died without making a sound.

The second needle was already between Baian's teeth, and he nodded to Hikojiro again.

Hikojiro plastered a sheet of paper over the face of the samurai sleeping in the middle while Baian plunged the needle into his heart. The man shuddered briefly then he, too, lay still.

Suddenly the third samurai mumbled something in his sleep and turned onto his side. Baian and Hikojiro retreated to the corner of the room, keeping a close watch on their prey.

When the man lay still and began to snore, Hikojiro returned to his position by the pillow. The third needle was ready. Hikojiro readied the wet paper and lifted it up in both hands. Baian nodded for the third time, reached out with his left hand, and turned the man onto his back.

The samurai's eyes opened, but before he could move, Hikojiro slapped the paper over his face and Baian's needle flashed in the dull light of the lantern.

❖ ❖ ❖

By the time the bodies were found in the morning by one of the maids, Baian and Hikojiro had already walked as far as Kusatsu. Baian had left the money for their room as well as a generous tip.

Thick clouds covered the sky, and the morning air was cool. They hurried through Kusatsu without a word, heading for Mekawa. When they arrived at the inn where on that first day they had eaten the grilled tofu, they found the front door still closed.

"Wait here please, Hiko," Baian said. He walked around to the rear of the building, went into the kitchen, and asked a servant girl to fetch the owner.

"Why, if it isn't Dr. Kyoan from Otsu," the old man said happily.

147

"Has Kaneko been buried?"

"Yes."

"What was his connection with the village?"

Suspicion clouded the landlord's face for a moment, but when he had decided that Baian did not mean any harm he replied, "His mother was born here."

Baian nodded. He had guessed that Kaneko was the illegitimate son of a maid who had gone to work for the Kaneko family. The *ronin* must have inherited the family name because there was no legitimate heir.

"Is Kyuma still at the Kaneko house?"

"Yes, why?"

Baian produced a parcel from his kimono. It contained fifty pieces of gold and a letter. "I would appreciate it if you would give him this."

"Where will you be?"

"I have urgent business in Edo, but he'll know what to do with it."

The landlord did not know what was going on, but he could see that Baian was not going to take no for an answer. He took the parcel.

"Thank you and goodbye." Baian hurried back to where Hikojiro was waiting. "It's done."

He put on his hat, and the two of them hurried away.

The letter for Kyuma read:

> *Leave the house as soon as possible; the enemy know where you are. Use the money as you see fit.*
> *Omura Kyoan*

Baian and Hikojiro hurried down the road, hoping to cross the Suzuka Pass before nightfall.

"Hiko, can you smell chrysanthemums?"

"No. But you have a keener sense of smell than I do."

"I'm looking forward to getting back to Edo."

"Me too. But what do you think will happen to Kyuma?"

"I have no idea."

"Do you think they'll send more people after him?"

"I should imagine so."

They continued to walk without slowing their pace.

"We did what we could for him," Baian said, "but nothing is to be gained by us poking our noses any further into the matter. After this, we must leave him to his fate."

NEW YEAR'S NOODLES

It was such a cold, gray December morning that Baian thought it might snow later on that day. He and Hikojiro had returned from their trip to Kyoto the previous evening.

"Why don't you stay the night?" Baian offered.

"No thanks," Hikojiro replied. "I know it's not much of a house and there's nobody waiting there for me, but now that I'm back in Edo, I realize how much I missed my place." And he set off toward the small house he rented from a temple in Asakusa.

❖ ❖ ❖

I expect Baian will be starting to see his patients today, Hikojiro thought with a smile. He was preparing a dish he was very partial to for breakfast—a bowl of plain rice gruel in fish stock.

When they returned to Edo after their stay in Kyoto, Baian and Hikojiro had about ten gold pieces left in their purses.

"Let's try to make this last until the end of the year," Baian said.

"Yes, I'd like to earn some honest money, at least until I can get the smell of blood off my hands," Hikojiro agreed.

❖ ❖ ❖

The unheated house was freezing cold. Hikojiro eagerly sat down to eat the steaming rice gruel, in which he had used the small amount of soy sauce he had in the kitchen to bring out the flavor of the fish stock.

The whole house was covered with six months' worth of dust, and he realized that he had a good two days' hard work ahead of him before the place was habitable again. His first task, however, was to go to his wife's grave to tell her that he had avenged her for the humiliation that had driven her to kill their baby daughter and then commit suicide.

The grave was at a temple in Magome. In the many years since her death, he had never neglected to visit it.

I'll be forty-three soon, he thought in amazement. He had never expected to live so long.

The death of his wife and daughter had been indirectly responsible for his becoming a hired killer. There were many people in the world who deserved to die—like the two *ronin* who had caused his wife's death—but who somehow had managed to escape punishment. These were the only kind of people that a worthy assassin was supposed to kill, and it was this that appealed to his sense of justice.

He planned to visit his wife's grave first, then tidy the house and do some shopping, before going to ask the local tofu shop to resume its regular morning deliveries. He had been on his own for so many years now that he did not find these domestic chores irksome; rather, it felt good to get back into his old routines. He hoped to be able to concentrate on his trade for the time being, at least until he managed to forget the recent deaths he had caused.

After eating breakfast, he donned a narrow-sleeved kimono and fastened the sash tightly.

"Excuse me," someone said from the front of the house. "Is Hikojiro at home?"

"Who is it?"

"Kyubei sent me."

"The door's open."

The man who came into the house was in his mid-thirties and very fat. "I was told to give you this," he said, handing Hikojiro a letter.

Hikojiro recognized Kyubei's handwriting on the envelope and realized right away that it must mean another contract to kill. He frowned before breaking open the seal. The short letter consisted of an invitation to the Tamaya Restaurant in Asakusa at two o'clock that afternoon. Kyubei obviously did not know that Hikojiro had been out of town for the past six months.

Kyubei's Offer

The Tamaya's specialty was clam soup, but Hikojiro much preferred the nearby Miyoshiya's version of the same dish.

Hikojiro decided to put off the visit to his wife's grave until the next day. It would not have mattered if he had been out when the messenger came, but having received the letter in person, he could not afford to be late for the meeting.

Kyubei ran a firm that found servants for the samurai and lords living in the Kanda area. Four other companies were in the same business in Edo, but Kyubei's was by far the biggest and oldest. The firm had been in his family for five generations, and many of the samurai clans had used its services since its establishment. He was approximately the same age as Hikojiro, but whereas Hikojiro looked much older than his years, Kyubei looked younger.

Having so many connections with the nobility, he was probably one of the most powerful bosses in the city. Although Hikojiro had no way of knowing just how powerful he really was, he knew better than to be late when Kyubei summoned him.

❖ ❖ ❖

Kyubei was waiting in a private room on the second floor of the Tamaya.

"How have you been doing, Hiko?" Kyubei asked jovially. "You look as if you've put on a bit of weight."

"Really?" Hikojiro did not say anything about his trip to Kyoto.

A waitress appeared with some *sake*. They sat in silence until she left.

"I know I needn't tell you why I've asked you to come here today."

"I take it you want a job done."

"Exactly. I know you must be very busy, what with the end of the year approaching, but I'm afraid my client is in a hurry to get this job done."

"I had hoped to have a bit of time off from this kind of work, but as it's you, I can hardly refuse, can I?" Hikojiro said with a wry grin. "After all, I still owe you one."

"I don't mean to take advantage of you. It's just that I don't know anyone else who could handle this job."

Two years earlier Kyubei had paid him an advance of twenty-five gold pieces for a job, but Hikojiro had fallen sick and been unable to fulfill the contract. Kyubei, how-ever, had not demanded the advance payment back. On the contrary, he told Hikojiro to keep the money for his medical expenses. Kyubei's generosity had saved Hikojiro's life, and Hikojiro felt deeply in his debt.

"Will you do it then?" Kyubei asked. The gentle expres-sion on his face was betrayed by a light shining deep in his eyes. He placed a purse containing twenty-five gold pieces on the table between them.

"You needn't do that. I've still got the money you gave me last time. Just pay the remainder when I've finished the job."

"Don't be stupid. I told you, that was a present."

"But…"

"Come on, take it."

"All right, if you insist."

If a hired killer took money for nothing, he might feel obliged later on to take on a job that he would otherwise have declined. But Kyubei had been so insistent that Hiko-jiro had accepted. That a professional killer of Hikojiro's standing had allowed himself to come under obligation to a go-between showed just how much he trusted Kyubei.

"I know I needn't ask, but…"

"What is it?"

"The victim does deserves to die, doesn't he?"

"As you said yourself, it goes without saying. You don't think I'd be involved otherwise, do you?"

"I'm sorry, I just like to be quite sure about these things."

"I understand."

The two spent the rest of the afternoon talking. As evening fell, a palanquin arrived to pick up Kyubei. Leaving, he said, "Your target is a dangerous man. Be careful."

"I thought you said it was a rush job."

"Yes. The client wants it done by the end of the year. That's why I came to you. But if you know anyone you can trust, an accomplice or two might come in useful."

"No, I'll do it on my own."

"All right, but be as quick as you can."

"Leave it to me."

A Winter Supper

Hikojiro left home early the next morning. The sky remained overcast, but the snow still held off. He went first to visit his wife's grave in Magome, then to Baian's house.

When Hikojiro arrived, Baian was in the living room cleaning his needles.

"You know, I think that nearly every patient I've ever had must have been waiting for me to get back. I've been rushed off my feet all day. I haven't even had time for a pipe. It's difficult to get back into the swing of things after a six-month break."

"I bought a bottle of *sake* on my way over."

"You're a godsend, Hiko. I won't be long. Why don't you warm yourself by the brazier?"

"No, that's all right, I'll warm the *sake*."

"Thanks. While you're in the kitchen, could you make some fish stock?"

"Of course. What's it for?"

"I was going to make a clam and white radish stew."

Hikojiro went to the kitchen and started to prepare the stock.

"Where have you been today?" Baian asked.

"I went to visit my wife's grave."

"And after that?"

"Oh, here and there."

"You've taken on another job, haven't you?"

"How did you know? Is it that obvious?"

"I could tell easily enough."

"Kyubei asked me to do it," Hikojiro admitted. After having spent six months on the road with Baian, he knew he could trust him implicitly.

"And who's the victim?"

"A *ronin* of about thirty. I had a look at him this afternoon. He's a huge man, covered with thick black hair —looks just like the famous robber Ishikawa Goemon."

"Sounds like a tough one."

"Kyubei told me that he was employed by an official called Shimada over in Hamacho until last summer."

"I suppose that Kyubei probably met a man like Shimada through his business."

"More than likely."

"And how does the job look?"

"I don't know. I think I'd better watch him a bit longer before making up my mind."

"Does he live alone?"

"Yes. In a small house in Jumokudani in Shirogane."

"Not far from here then."

"That's why I dropped in on my way home. But I'd never realized how spooky Jumokudani is."

"It was an execution ground in the old days. It was called Hell Valley then."

"I'd never heard that before," Hikojiro said. "That explains it."

Night closed in. The two men sat around the brazier on top of which they placed an earthenware pot full of the stock prepared by Hikojiro. Next to the brazier were two bamboo baskets, one containing sliced white radish and the other clams. When the stock came to the boil, Baian picked up one handful of radish and one of clams and dropped them into the simmering stock. The thinly sliced radish and shellfish were soon cooked. Baian served two generous bowls of stew, and they started to eat, blowing on the soup to cool it.

"This is great, Baian."

"It's hard to beat, especially in winter."

They drank *sake* from tea bowls.

"By the way, Hiko," Baian said between mouthfuls. "Tell me a bit more about your job."

"As I'm doing it for Kyubei I didn't ask for any details. But one look at the guy's face, and it's easy to imagine that he must have given his old master a lot of trouble. I suppose a man like Shimada can't risk the scandal of killing the *ronin* himself. That's probably why he got in touch with Kyubei. He can save a lot of fuss that way."

"You're probably right."

"I think I've had too much to drink."

"Would you like some rice now?"

"Yes, please."

"Why don't you stay the night?"

"Yes, I think I'd better."

Baian served two bowls of freshly cooked white rice, onto which he poured the remainder of the stew. Stirring the rice into the soup, they ate it greedily with a side dish of pickled vegetables.

"Hiko."

"What?"

"It's started to snow."

Baian's senses were so finely honed that even the silent fall of snowflakes could not escape his notice.

The Mysterious Patient

Hikojiro left Baian's house late the following morning.

The snow had passed during the night, hardly settling at all. A weak sun shone in the sky.

Even before Hikojiro left, patients began to appear at Baian's doorstep. He had a reputation in the area for being a first-class doctor, and because his fees were low, he never had a shortage of patients.

Baian worked hard until two o'clock, when he paused for lunch. He sent Oseki home after she had cleared the dishes. Shortly afterwards he had a visitor.

"Good afternoon," said a gruff voice.

Baian went to the front door and found a short, elderly man standing outside, his grey head bowed. He could tell at a glance that the man must be a temple servant.

"What can I do for you? Are you sick?"

"No, it's not me."

"Oh? Where's the patient?"

"We were told that you're an excellent doctor, and the abbot sent me to ask if you could help us."

"Where is your temple?"

"The Jozaiji in Shirogane."

"Can't the patient come here?"

"No, I am afraid she can't be moved."

"What's wrong with her?"

"Several things."

Baian could read a silent plea not to ask any more questions in the old man's eyes.

"All right. Wait here."

"Thank you. I'm terribly grateful."

"You don't have to thank me. It's my job."

Baian collected his equipment and locked up. The old man led the way, carrying Baian's bag.

They walked for some time until they came to a small temple backed by a bamboo grove. As they turned into the narrow path leading to the gate, Baian suddenly stopped and looked back.

He's still following us, Baian thought.

Someone had tailed them all the way from Shinagawa, but he was not very good at it, and Baian had sensed his presence at once. He was a huge man, who wore a broad-rimmed hat that hid his face. Although he was fashionably dressed, Baian could tell at a glance that he was a *ronin*.

When Baian glanced back, the man leaned against the wall of a neighboring mansion, nonchalantly feigning innocence.

Baian's whole body tensed. Like Hikojiro, he had killed countless men and women during his career. Now there was no knowing who might want to kill him.

Turning back to the old servant waiting for him, Baian saw that he too was staring at the gigantic *ronin* with apprehension.

The old man knows who he is, Baian realized.

It seemed safe to assume that the *ronin* had some connection with the temple. Baian wondered if this had anything to do with his patient.

"Let's go," he said to the servant, and followed him up the path to the temple gate.

All the buildings in the temple compound, from the gate and bell tower to the main hall and priests' quarters, were thatched, which gave the place a pleasant, rural aspect. There were very few other houses in this part of Shirogane, and the temple stood alone in the fields. It had been built one hundred and eighty years earlier, which made it an old temple by Edo standards.

The patient lay in a darkened room at the back of the main hall. It was a young woman. Another servant and a young priest were with her.

Although dark, the room was warm, and the smell of medicine hung in the air. Baian began his examination.

"Why was she left until she reached this condition?" he asked.

The young priest bowed his head and exchanged a look with the old servant, but neither answered.

"This is deplorable."

The girl had a beautiful pale complexion, but she was so undernourished that her body had withered to skin and bones. Bruises stood out on her shrivelled breasts, and she had been savagely beaten around the back and stomach. Someone had applied ointment to her wounds and given her medicine, but the injuries were much too severe for that to have had any effect. He did not know why a doctor had not been called earlier, but he realized that there must be a good reason.

She had also sustained serious internal injuries, and was in great pain. She frowned and shut her eyes tightly during Baian's examination.

Every time he asked "Does this hurt?" she would answer with a slight nod or shake of the head. As he probed her injuries with his fingers, a moan would escape from her lips when she could no longer bear the pain.

Baian took out his needles and began to tend her wounds. He worked for several hours. By the time he finished he was drenched with sweat. After the treatment the girl was able to fall asleep. Baian heard a sigh of admiration come from behind. Turning, he saw that the young priest and servant had gone, and an elderly priest with a long white beard was kneeling on the floor behind him. Baian guessed that this must be the abbot of the temple.

"Thank you very much for all you have done," the old man said with a deep bow.

"How did you hear about me?"

"The abbot of Sofukuji temple recommended you."

Sofukuji was near Baian's house. Every time he fell ill, the elderly abbot would refuse to be treated by anyone but Baian.

"The abbot spoke very highly of your character as well as your skill as a doctor, so I thought I would take the chance and call you in."

"Take the chance?"

"Yes."

The old priest did nothing to allay Baian's suspicions, and neither did he elaborate. Baian knew that there was some secret here, but he did not ask any more. It had nothing to do with him; his only concern was to make sure that the injured girl made a full recovery. As he left the sickroom, he turned to the abbot and said, "I won't mention this to anyone."

The old priest nodded gravely, then bowed again, his hands clasped in front of him as if in prayer.

Baian made his way out of the main hall, watched by the young priest and the servant. When he reached the temple gate he caught a brief glimpse of the top of a straw hat, as its owner ducked behind the bell tower.

It's the *ronin*. He is still watching me.

Pretending not to have noticed, Baian walked through the gate. When he reached the end of the path, however, instead of turning left to go home, he turned right.

Once around the corner, he looked back to check that nobody was in sight, then he broke into a run. When he had built up enough speed, he jumped to the top of the wall of a neighboring mansion. The branches of an old pine tree stretched over to the wall and provided him with an ideal hiding place.

It was a cloudy winter day, and dusk was near.

Suddenly the *ronin* appeared. Assuming that Baian was going home, he turned left in the direction of the main road.

Baian watched from his vantage point on top of the wall, and as soon as the man had disappeared, he jumped down into the street again.

Now it's my turn.

Turning the Tables

Baian's shortest route home would take him south through Shirogane, until he reached the narrow Shina-gawadai Road. The *ronin* did not realize that he had lost Baian until he reached the main road. He then stopped for a moment and looked around. He did not seem to be very upset about losing his prey, and after a short while he turned and walked back the way he had come.

Baian watched all this from an alleyway between two shops. After the *ronin* had walked past, Baian started to follow him.

It was now quite dark, which made it both easier and harder to follow the *ronin*. Although Baian would be less likely to be seen, his prey was not carrying a lantern and Baian could not afford to keep too much distance between himself and the *ronin*.

The man walked along without so much as a glance back. He continued to the end of the road, then turned left in the direction of Jumokudani.

It can't be! Baian thought. But no matter how hard he tried to deny it, he could not shake the idea that this was the man Hikojiro had been hired to kill. Everything Hiko-jiro had told him about the *ronin* seemed to fit. He was even heading in the direction of the place where Hikojiro said he lived. It just could not be, Baian said to himself again.

Despite his efforts, Baian's feeling continued to grow by the minute. Finally, he watched the huge man enter a small hut in the woods of Jumokudani. He did not light a lamp after he had gone in.

Baian made his way through the woods toward the building. He was careful not to make any sound that might betray his presence.

I wonder what's going on? Hikojiro was hired to kill this *ronin*, so why should he be tailing me?

If the man had somehow found out that Hikojiro was planning to kill him, it would be understandable if he were to tail Hikojiro, but why bother with Baian?

I can't believe that there could be two people like him living around here—which means that he must be Hikojiro's target, Baian speculated. But what should I do now? Anyway, I think I'll try to get a look at his face, just to make sure.

The man still had not lit a lamp, so Baian was not quite sure how he was going to manage even that. He crept silently toward the hut and saw that there was only one entrance.

A cold wind whistled through the treetops, and Baian could have sworn that he heard a voice. The wind dropped, and sure enough the voice came again.

"Excuse me. You out there," the man in the house called. Baian did not move from his hiding place, nor did he answer.

"You are a big man, too. It must be hard for you to crouch down like that."

Baian still said nothing.

"You needn't worry. I didn't mean you any harm when I

166

followed you this afternoon. Please accept my apologies."

The man spoke in a whisper, but it carried clearly to Baian.

"I just wanted to see for myself what kind of man you were before you went to tend the girl at the temple."

"Why?" Baian asked, speaking for the first time.

"I lost you halfway, but I wanted to follow you until you got home."

"Why?" Baian asked again.

"It would be rather awkward for me if you were to tell anyone about what you saw today."

"Go on."

"When I was halfway back, I realized that I was being followed, and I guessed it must be you. Anyway, why don't you come in? I have nothing to gain by keeping you in the dark any longer, and it might help the girl if you knew a bit more about her story."

"In that case, I'll come in."

"I'm sorry, I couldn't light a lamp even if I wanted to."

"It's all the same to me."

Having made up his mind, Baian got up and went into the house.

He spent that night in the *ronin*'s house. He did not sleep, but listened to the *ronin*'s story until dawn began to brighten the eastern sky. The room held nothing but sleeping quilts and *sake*, and the *ronin* shared both with Baian. They sat, wrapped in the quilts, drinking as they talked. Early the following day Baian returned home to Shinagawadai.

When Oseki arrived that morning, she found Baian dressed and ready to go out.

"I won't be back for two or three days," he told her as he left.

He walked as far as the main crossroads, where he hired a palanquin.

"To Asakusa. As fast as you can," he said, giving the bearers a generous tip.

They set off at full speed, and some time later they arrived in front of Hikojiro's house. Hikojiro was still at home.

"Hiko! I was worried you might be out," Baian said, relieved to find his friend.

"I was just about to go out to watch the *ronin* again."

"He knows you were watching him the other night."

"What? How do you know that?"

"I met him last night."

"But Baian, you—"

"You're right, he is a frightening-looking man. He looks like a giant toad. But you should never judge people on appearances—he's basically a very good man."

"But how...?"

"Do you remember mentioning that you thought he resembled the famous robber Ishikawa? Well you weren't too far off the mark. His surname really is Ishikawa."

"What?"

"His first name is Tomogoro."

"What is all this about, Baian?"

"I was surprised, I can tell you."

"Come on, spit it out. What have you been up to?"

"Can you fix me something to eat first? I rushed out without having any breakfast. I'm starving."

"Well, all right. We'll talk later."

Hikojiro looked very ill at ease when he went into the kitchen. He heated up some soup, broke two eggs into a bowl, and brought everything on a tray with some rice and pickles.

"Will that be all right?"

"All right? It's a feast."

Baian poured the eggs over the rice and swallowed the whole bowlful in a matter of seconds. He ate the second bowl of rice a bit more slowly with the soup and pickles.

"Have you got any tea?"

"Come on, tell me your story."

Later the two of them went to the Izutsu Restaurant, where they sat in Baian's usual room, drinking *sake* as they talked.

When evening fell, Hikojiro got up to leave. "Tomorrow then," he said, and made his way back to his house.

Kyubei's Story

Next morning the weather was fine. When Baian awoke in his room at the Izutsu, Omoto was no longer in bed beside him. It was the first time in six months they had slept together. He had not even had to ask her to come—as soon as darkness fell, she had gone straight to his room.

"I couldn't wait any longer," Omoto said. "I've thought of nothing but you for the last six months."

"I've been away on a trip."

"I heard."

The once plump Omoto had lost a lot of weight and now looked almost slim.

"Did you have an affair with anyone else while I was away?"

"I wish I could, but I'm not that kind of woman."

She reached out hesitatingly, embraced him, and nibbled his earlobe. She had not been the same since Baian had first taken her to bed, and the restaurant kitchen where she worked was full of rumors.

The bed was still filled with her smell and the perfume

of her hair oil. Baian sat up and slapped his forehead. He had almost forgotten about his patient at the Jozaiji. Jumping out of bed, he clapped his hands to call Omoto.

"I want you to call a palanquin to take me to Shirogane. Don't worry, I'll be back soon."

He realized that he had missed Omoto's warm, soft body during the time they were apart. He usually preferred younger women, but recently they did not seem to excite him as before.

At around the same time that Baian left the Izutsu, Kyubei summoned Hikojiro to his private room at the Tamaya Restaurant.

"I was in the neighborhood so I thought I'd drop by and see how you were getting on," Kyubei said. "Have you seen him yet, Hikojiro?"

"Yes, briefly."

"Does it look like a tricky job?"

"Yes, it won't be easy."

"That's why I came to you. I don't care how you go about it, as long as you get it done. You have ways of doing these things that I can only guess at, isn't that so?"

"Well—" Hikojiro gave a weak smile, and this seemed enough to put Kyubei's fears to rest.

"You do a good job and you can have an extra twenty gold pieces as a bonus."

"Thank you."

"And when do you think you'll be able to finish it?"

"I'm not sure yet."

"Lord Shimada is in a hurry."

"I don't like to ask, but could you fill me in a bit about what he's done? It might help me come up with a way to deal with him. It will be very difficult to get close to him unless I know what his weaknesses are. After all, I'm working alone, and he seems to be on his guard all the time. He's so strong that maybe it would be best if you were to find another samurai to do the job instead."

"He's already killed the two samurai I sent after him," Kyubei said with a rare flash of irritation. "Two of my best men. They were both excellent swordsmen, and neither had ever lost a fight, but they were no match for him. That's why I came to you, Hikojiro. I knew I could rely on you." Kyubei gave him a searching look. "You realize, of course, that now I've told you this much, it's too late to turn the job down."

"You still haven't told me anything."

"Well, his name is Ishikawa Tomogoro. Five years ago Lord Shimada took him off the streets and gave him a job. But he forgot his debt and turned against his master."

According to Kyubei, Tomogoro had an affair with the wife of Shimada's steward, and it ended with him murdering her. Not content with that, he raped the steward's daughter and then abducted her.

"So now you know why he deserves to die," Kyubei concluded.

"But if that's the case, why doesn't Lord Shimada just inform the police? He knows where he's hiding."

"I've told you all I know," Kyubei replied in a quiet voice. "When I heard the story I realized that the man did not deserve to live, and so I agreed to take on the job. You shouldn't push your luck, you know. You can turn down this job if you want, but I don't think you'll have long to live if you do."

This was not a threat, it was a fact. Kyubei might be having trouble getting rid of Tomogoro, but Hikojiro would be a simple job—and nobody knew this better than Hikojiro himself.

"I never said that I didn't want to do it. You have nothing to worry about."

"In that case can you give me a date when it will be finished?"

Hikojiro thought for a moment.

"I'll do it by the end of the year." Then he asked, "I take it that nobody knows about this but you and I?"

"Of course. That's the rule."

The Shogun's Adviser

By the time Hikojiro had returned home and changed his clothes, Baian was in the room at Jozaiji Temple, treating his patient.

"I could hardly believe it, doctor, she actually ate some gruel this morning," the old servant said.

After Baian finished the treatment, the old man left the room to fetch some hot water with which Baian could wash up.

As soon as he was alone with the girl, Baian knelt and whispered into her ear, "Your name is Ochie, isn't it?"

The girl's eyes opened in surprise.

"There's no need to worry. Tomogoro told me the whole story."

"Is he…"

"You must not tell anyone about it, all right? Tomogoro is safe, so don't worry about him."

"But…"

"You must sleep now, you are still very weak." He began to wipe the perspiration from her body with a white cotton towel.

With another two weeks of treatment, Baian thought as he looked down on her emaciated frame, she should get her appetite back. After that, it won't be long before she puts on weight again and her body fills out as a twenty-year-old's should.

As he left the temple, the abbot bowed again and, giving an embarrassed bow in return, Baian hurried through the gate.

❖ ❖ ❖

Just about the time Baian was leaving the temple, Kyubei was in a secret meeting with a well-dressed samurai at a restaurant in the pleasure quarter of Yanagibashi. Two servants had arrived with the samurai, but they had been ordered to wait in another room.

The samurai had been wearing a hood when he entered the room, but he removed it now to reveal his face. He was a tall, arrogant-looking man in his mid-forties. He had thin eyebrows over large, piercing eyes, an aquiline nose, and a rather large mouth with a protruding lower lip.

"I can guarantee that the matter will be cleared up by the end of the year, my lord," Kyubei said with a deferential bow.

"It had better be."

The samurai was Lord Shimada, one of the shogun's ten personal advisers and consequently a power in the land. Although his rank was not very high by birth, his appointment as one of the shogun's advisers meant that there was no telling how high he might rise in the world. Even the highest officials of the shogun's court thought twice before crossing him.

"What kind of man have you sent after Ishikawa?" Shimada demanded.

"You needn't worry yourself about that, my lord. Leave it to me."

"If you need more money, I can afford to let you have a

little more, but you must have Ishikawa killed quickly," he said arrogantly. "If you do a good job, you will find me a grateful man."

"Thank you, my lord."

Shimada could give Kyubei a monopoly to supply all workers for government contracts. The amount of money that would involve was enough to make even Kyubei's mind boggle.

"I hope you realize the position I'm in."

"Of course, my lord."

"That's why I cannot afford any mistakes. As long as Ishikawa stays in Edo, I can't move against him myself. Of course if he were to leave and hide somewhere else in the country, I could deal with it without your help."

"I quite understand, my lord."

"He's staying in Edo just to spite me." His face twisted with anger and he beat the edge of the brazier with his fan. "I hate him. I don't want him to live for one more day."

"Leave everything to me, my lord."

A short while later, Shimada left the restaurant, his face once again hidden by his hood. He signalled to the lacquered palanquin that was waiting out of sight, and set off for his mansion.

❖ ❖ ❖

The following morning Hikojiro turned up at Baian's house.

"I managed to bump into one of Shimada's servants at a gambling den. After I bought him a few drinks and lent him some money, he became very talkative."

"Really?"

"Yes, and I managed to get the whole story out of him."

"What story?"

"It would appear that Lord Shimada is a fiend. He's unable to control his appetites and often goes out into the streets in disguise and attacks hostesses in restaurants."

"I see."

"I managed to hear something else that might come in useful."

"What?"

"The 28th of this month is the anniversary of his father's death."

"Oh?"

"Yes. He's buried at a temple in Hijiri, and if Shimada is not in attendance on the shogun, he always attends a memorial service there on that day."

"The 28th, you say?"

"That's right."

"Do you intend to go through with this?"

"I don't have a choice anymore."

"These days we seem to spend most of our time working for free."

"Yes. I'm sorry that I've had to involve you like this again."

"We've got to be quite sure about this before we start."

"I know, but we don't have any choice."

❖ ❖ ❖

The next day Ishikawa disappeared from the house in Jumokudani.

A week passed. Baian, looking after all his patients, worked like a man possessed.

"It's good to see you back to your old self, doctor," Oseki said. "It makes it worth coming here to work everyday."

"That's a relief. I couldn't bear to live a single day without you."

"It does an old woman's heart good to hear things like that, even if you don't mean them. I'll tell you what—shall I slip out later tonight and come to see you—just the two of us?"

"I'd love you to, but I have to think of your reputation."

Hikojiro was out of his house nearly every day, and he never returned until nightfall. One evening at about eight o'clock, a boy from the Tamaya Restaurant appeared at his door.

"Kyubei wants to see you."

"Tell him I'll be over right away."

After the boy left, Hikojiro sat deep in thought for a time. Then he washed his face, carefully combed his hair, and changed his clothes before setting out for the meeting.

When he arrived, he found Kyubei waiting in his usual room.

"I happened to be in the neighborhood, so I thought to see you and find out how the job is progressing. Don't get me wrong, I'm not trying to rush you. I know that once you've taken on a job, it's as good as done, but as I said, I happened to be in the vicinity."

Hikojiro nodded slowly. There was something final about the gesture.

"Kyubei."

"Yes?" Kyubei leaned forward.

"I'd like to meet you on the 27th to receive the remainder of the money."

"Do you really mean it?"

"Yes, don't worry."

"So you have a plan then."

"Yes, but I don't want to meet you here. In the future, I don't really want to be seen with you in any of the restaurants around here."

"What is that supposed to mean?"

"This is my local neighborhood, and the kind of business we are involved in ..."

Kyubei slapped his knee.

"Of course. I'm sorry."

"We are talking about murder."

"I know, I'm sorry, but you're sure about the 27th, are you?"

"Yes, I'll finish the job on the evening of the 26th. I'll come to see you on the 27th, so if you could send someone over to verify Ishikawa's death ...."

"There'll be no need for that. The moment Ishikawa's dead, I'll hear about it. We needn't bother with formalities."

"It's just that this time I'll be using a rather unusual technique," Hikojiro said with a grin. "And I thought you might be interested to see how I do it." His confidence showed in his smile.

"Oh, I see," Kyubei said excitedly. "You mean you won't be using a knife?"

"Of course not."

"How about poison?"

"Don't talk nonsense. He's not the kind of man who's likely to fall for poison. Just you wait and see. But where should I meet you to get the money?"

"Do you know a restaurant called the Kameya in Yanagi-bashi?"

"By reputation."

"Why don't you come at noon—if that's not too early?"

"Not at all, it will be fine."

"We can have lunch together."

"Thanks. I'll see you later then."

"Yes. Here take this, it's not much, but I want you to

have it anyway," Kyubei said, holding out a small purse of money.

An Appointment with Death

The morning of the 27th dawned. The sky was heavy with the threat of snow.

Baian had been staying at the Izutsu since the previous morning. Shortly before lunch he ordered a palanquin to take him out.

He wore a long, yellow-checked kimono, a black jacket embroidered with his family crest, and white *tabi* socks. His head was freshly shaved, and covered with a pale greenish-yellow cloth hat. He had wrapped a white silk scarf around his neck and looked like a wealthy doctor.

He took the palanquin across the Ryogoku Bridge to the east bank of the river.

"I'll walk the rest of the way, thank you."

He waited until the palanquin was out of sight, then crossed back over the river to Asakusa. He was carrying a small parcel under his arm.

Baian walked to Yanagibashi and walked into the Kameya Restaurant.

"Could I trouble you for some *sake* and something to eat?" he asked, slipping the maid a large tip. "I was just passing, I hope it won't be too much trouble."

He removed his expensive sandals by the front door.

Although the Kameya did not usually cater to casual diners, they were always ready to make an exception for someone of Baian's apparent wealth and status.

He was shown to a small private room facing the garden where he ordered a light lunch. When the food arrived, he drank the soup and sipped a little *sake,* packing the rest into a box he had brought with him. He could not eat much now for fear that it might interfere with what he had come to do.

A few moments later Baian saw Kyubei being led to a room on the opposite side of the garden. He was grateful for this because it saved him the trouble of looking for him.

A short while later he rose and hid his parcel in a cupboard. Slipping on a pair of garden clogs, he crossed the garden to Kyubei's room. Nobody noticed him leave his room.

Inside, Kyubei was waiting impatiently for Hikojiro to arrive. Baian slid open the door silently and slipped inside.

"Who are you? What do you want?" Kyubei asked, putting down his *sake* cup.

"Hikojiro sent me," Baian replied, crossing the distance between them and sitting next to Kyubei. "I have something confidential to tell you."

"Hikojiro?" Kyubei repeated, turning the side of his head toward Baian. As he did so, Baian's right hand shot out, grabbed him by the throat, and squeezed a vital nerve.

Kyubei slumped into unconsciousness with little more than a whimper. Baian reached into the front of his kimono to draw out a needle, which he put between his teeth. He had slipped a leather ring onto his finger before he had entered the room. Taking the needle from his mouth, he drove it into the nape of Kyubei's neck, forcing it upward until it reached the brain. Kyubei twitched once, then lay still. There was virtually no blood.

Baian returned to his room, removed the parcel of food from the cupboard, and called the waitress for the bill. By the time he left the restaurant, the first flakes of snow had begun to fall.

One hour before, Hikojiro had appeared at Kyubei's office in Mikawacho. "I would like to see Kyubei as soon as possible. It's urgent," he said to the clerk.

"I'm afraid the boss is out at the moment."

"Where's he gone?"

"I don't know, but he said that he'd be back in about two hours."

The clerk apparently did not know of Kyubei's appointment with Hikojiro.

"In that case I'll wait, if that's all right."

"Of course, you're welcome to," the clerk said, but secretly he thought, What can he want with the boss? He's only a toothpick maker and a bit out of his league here.

After he had waited about an hour, Hikojiro rose to his feet.

"I'll come again."

"Do you want to leave a message?"

"No, just tell him that I was here."

He knew that Kyubei's body would have been found by now, and that the restaurant would be in confusion, but at least he could prove that he had been nowhere near the scene at the time of death.

Tying Up Loose Ends

At eight o'clock the following morning, Lord Shimada left the mansion in his official palanquin to visit his family temple and pray for his father's soul. He was accompanied by his son, four retainers, and two servants. He always made a point of visiting the temple on the anniversaries of his ancestors' deaths if he was not in attendance on the shogun.

Edo was covered with a thin layer of snow, but the snow had stopped before settling properly. The sky was dark and still, and the air was very cold.

In addition to being an extremely ambitious man, Lord Shimada also lacked all control over his sexual appetites.

One day he had come across the wife of his steward—whose family had served his own for generations—dragged her into a storehouse, and raped her. Unable to recover from the experience, she hanged herself. She was forty-five at the time and not particularly attractive, which showed the depths of Shimada's depravity.

The steward pretended not to know what had happened, not out of any feelings of loyalty, but simply because he did not have the nerve to stand up to his master.

Next, Shimada had come across the steward's daughter, Ochie, and forced her into the storehouse. Ochie had put up a fight, and Shimada had beaten her viciously before raping her and leaving her locked in the storehouse.

It was Ishikawa Tomogoro who had rescued her from the storeroom and carried her away in his arms.

That night in the house in Jumokudani, Ishikawa told Baian the whole story.

"I was born to a good family, but my father was an inveterate gambler. As a result my mother suffered a great deal before she died. A little while after her death, talk of my father's gambling debts and fighting came to the ears of the authorities, and we were stripped of our rank. A little later, my father committed suicide by jumping into the river. I was taken in by the priests of the Jozaiji.

"I've liked sword fighting ever since I was a child. Because I showed some aptitude for it, the abbot was able to find me a position with Lord Shimada. When Shimada learned of my skills, he took me everywhere as his bodyguard, but when I realized what kind of man he really was, he grew to disgust me.

"When he raped and half-killed Ochie, I could not stand by and watch any longer. I took Ochie to the temple, and came to live here, challenging Shimada by my presence. I meant to fight him, and I knew that he could not go to the police without wrecking his own career.

"Twice he has sent swordsmen to kill me, but I killed them both. Recently, a strange-looking man has been hanging around the house, but I'm not scared. I'll fight them all until I win."

Shimada soon found out where Ochie was hiding, but she was surrounded by priests. He could not do anything about her without getting into even worse trouble, so he had decided to start by getting rid of Ishikawa. That was when he got in touch with Kyubei.

Following the memorial service for his ancestors, Lord Shimada went to the toilet. The temple was icy cold, and he had to relieve himself before he going back to his mansion. He knew the building well and made his way along the corridor without a guide.

After finishing, he opened the door only to find his way blocked by a huge man dressed in a priest's robe.

"Excuse me," the priest said with a polite bow.

As Shimada pushed past, he gave a slight cry and froze, while Baian carried on down the corridor without looking back.

Baian had buried a needle deep into Shimada's skull. By the time the body was found, he had changed out of his disguise and was climbing the hill behind the temple.

❖ ❖ ❖

For the past three years Baian had gone to a famous restaurant in Akabane on New Year's Eve to eat the traditional New Year's noodles. This year he had invited Hikojiro to join him. Hikojiro arrived at Baian's house a little after noon, but before they could set out for the restaurant, the old servant and one of the priests from Jozaiji arrived with a large parcel.

"It's not much, but I'm afraid it's the most we can offer," the priest explained.

He produced a large pastry board, a rolling pin, a mound of buckwheat flour, and some fragrant Chinese lemons.

Baian and Hikojiro watched, dumbfounded, as the servant and priest went into the kitchen. The priest rolled out the dough and then cut it into thin strips with a large knife, to produce perfect noodles.

"We'll leave the rest to you."

"We look forward to seeing you in the New Year."

So saying, the two men left, with Baian and Hikojiro still at a loss for words.

"Well, that was a surprise."

"Yes, but at least we don't have to go all the way over to Akabane now."

"Yes, it was very good of them."

"Anyway, as they said, it's all up to us now, isn't it, Baian?"

The two started work and, later that evening, sat down to two bowls of steaming noodles.

"This is great."

"It's the country way of making them. I wouldn't be surprised if the abbot comes from Shinshu; the area is famous for its noodles. Now that I think about it, he did have a bit of an accent."

"I've got to hand it to you, Baian."

"I expect that Ishikawa is also eating noodles at the temple around now. And Ochie should be well enough to eat some, too."

"What do you think will happen to them?"

"I think they should go to Kyoto. I know some people

there who can look after them. If they stay there for about two years, it should be safe for them to return to Edo."

"But I'm in your debt again after this."

"Not at all, it's always give and take."

"I'd like to die for you one day."

"Don't talk nonsense."

"Why do you think Lord Shimada did what he did? A man in his position?"

"I suppose he was born that way—why else would he want to rape his steward's middle-aged wife? People who are born evil are the worst. They don't even know that they're doing wrong. It's a kind of disease, but one that even I can't cure with my needles. If you'd seen him praying at the temple, you would never have believed that he could be capable of what he did."

It grew dark. They drank, enjoying the silence of the night, until it was suddenly broken by the sound of the New Year's bell from the neighborhood temple.

"Hiko."

"What?"

"We managed to survive for another year."

"But what about next year?"

"Is the room warm enough?"

"Yes, it's fine."

"You can sleep where you are if you like."

"Well..."

"It's started snowing again, and it'll probably settle this time. Why don't you stay here for the holidays?"

"I think I might take you up on that."